OLIVER
NOCTURNE

Don't miss a night out with . . .

OLIVER NOCTURNE

THE VAMPIRE'S PHOTOGRAPH

THE SUNLIGHT SLAYINGS

BLOOD TIES

THE DEMON HUNTER

THE ETERNAL TOMB

OLIVER
NOCTURNE

THE
ETERNAL
TOMB

KEVIN EMERSON

SCHOLASTIC INC.

NEW YORK   TORONTO   LONDON   AUCKLAND   SYDNEY
MEXICO CITY   NEW DELHI   HONG KONG   BUENOS AIRES

ISBN-13: 978-0-545-05805-6
ISBN-10: 0-545-05805-8

12 11 10 9 8 7 6 5 4 3 2 1   9 10 11 12 13 14/0

Printed in the U.S.A.   40
First printing, April 2009

Contents

For Craig Walker and Michele Mortlock,
who first believed in Oliver

Prologue

By most measurements, Necresium was a small world. It consisted of only a few billion stars, a hundred wormholes, and eighteen planets that held life. That wasn't much compared to Necresium's closest neighboring world, where Earth was located, whose galaxies secretly contained thirty-one planets with alien ecosystems.

Necresium was located above, to the east, seventeen minutes earlier, and 8.2 gravity degrees away from Earth. It had little matter, and to humans it would have looked like a messy watercolor painting. They would never have understood that the long, fluttering bands of color were actually the brilliant, thousand-year-old Necresians.

There was, however, one being in Necresium that certain Earth creatures might have recognized. He owned a drug and alchemy emporium in one of the smaller cities. And he had just invited two guests to his shop for an important meeting.

< 1 >

The shopkeeper stood patiently behind a tall counter, watching the guests walk slowly down the aisle toward him. One woman was older, with long white hair. She was dressed in faded jeans, a long leather coat, and a cowboy hat, as if she'd just stepped out of the Wild West, which she had. The younger woman had wide, dark eyes and wore a flowing white gown and sandals, her hair braided, as if she'd just stepped out of ancient Greece, which was also true.

The younger guest held a diamond-shaped hand mirror with a jade border. She glanced to the wall behind the shopkeeper, where a similar mirror was hung on the wall. White lights seemed to dance in that mirror, as they also did in the one in her hand.

The guests' eyes darted around the shop, noting the neatly organized shelves of black bottles, the brightly lit ceiling, from which faint, tinny music played, and the tiled floor, on which their sandals and cowboy boots surprisingly made no sound.

Welcome, the shopkeeper said in their minds.

The guests paused, feeling a ripple of fear. The shopkeeper wasn't surprised. He had black, scaled skin, short yellow horns, a mouth of enormous saber teeth, and apple-size gold coin eyes. He also had ten legs and sixteen arms. The eight fingers on each hand came to long, razorlike points. He clicked them against the hard countertop, one then the next, like a slowly ticking clock.

Who are you? the younger guest thought to him.

I am Dexires. He smiled at her. *Have you enjoyed our gift?*

The young woman regarded the mirror in her hand. *I have. It — it's quite powerful.*

Of course.

Why did you ask us here? the older guest asked. She avoided looking at him.

I have something else for you, said Dexires. He placed a black bottle on the counter.

What is it? the older guest asked suspiciously.

Dexires didn't answer. Instead, he peered at the young woman and asked, *Do you know what I am?*

Yes, I believe I do, she answered.

And do you know what YOU are?

I —

It's not a trick question, Margaret.

Then . . . yes, Margaret Watkins answered.

Indeed, said Dexires, his smile widening, baring his glistening teeth fully. *Then you understand that what is about to happen on Earth, with the Nexia prophecy, must be stopped.*

Selene has delivered the key to undoing the prophecy to the vampire boy, said Margaret, nodding to the older guest.

And how did that go? asked Dexires.

Fine, said Selene. *Things got complicated, but*

luckily Oliver's older brother came along and helped relay my instructions.

Word has it that you were killed to raise the Artifact, said Dexires.

That's good to hear, said Selene. *We made it appear that I'd died and hid me in the past.*

It was very convincing. And are you enjoying Arcana? Dexires asked, referring to the town where Selene was hiding.

Well enough, said Selene.

There's something wrong, isn't there? Margaret asked worriedly.

Dexires nodded. *I'm afraid so. It's come to our attention that a certain party has taken an interest in the prophecy as well.*

Who? Margaret asked.

Well, unfortunately, one of us.

One of you? Selene asked. *How is that possible?*

Anything is possible, dear, said Dexires tightly. *Unfortunately, it was always a danger given the extreme effects of Finity in your world. But as a result, she has made things more complicated.*

Margaret's face paled. *Does she know about —*

Emalie? Dexires asked. *No, none of them do. Yet. But they will. . . . The dark portents still surround her. She has gotten closer to the vampire than we hoped, and thus closer to danger.*

Unless the prophecy is undone, said Margaret.

Yes, well, about that . . . Dexires opened the small bottle on the counter. A misty cloud rose from it and formed a picture before them.

Margaret and Selene gazed at the strange image, brows furrowed, as they tried to understand its meaning.

It's a backup, Dexires explained. *Just in case things don't go according to plan.* He closed the bottle and handed it to Margaret. *Free of charge. Now, it's time for you to go back.*

A shadow passed across Margaret's face.

Dexires's eyes glowed sympathetically. *Sister*, he thought to her affectionately, *you know what needs to be done.*

They're going to capture me when I return, said Margaret quietly.

Some things can't be avoided. And remember, that, too, is part of the plan.

Selene put an arm around Margaret's shoulder. *It will work*, she said.

But we can't be sure, and Emalie . . . A tear slipped from her eye.

Take comfort in this, Dexires advised. *No one is ever truly sure what is about to happen. So the playing field is level. Just make sure to use that mirror when the time is right. And as they say on Earth, good luck.*

Margaret nodded, slipping the bottle into her woven shoulder bag. She and Selene turned to leave.

Dexires watched them go, feeling guilty for what he'd just said. There was no such thing as good luck. Only what came next. What was fortunate for one being was almost always unfortunate for another. Such was the balance of the universe itself.

He turned to the mirror behind him. Many lights danced on his face. *It is all we can do*, he replied to them. Now the rest was in the hands of a few otherwise insignificant beings on Earth. Dexires smiled. It was always amusing how this universe worked. Hopefully it wouldn't end anytime soon.

Chapter 1

Infiltrating the Inquisition

*R*eady?

In the ink-black dead of night, a single red light flickered. Given its grave meaning, the light was surprisingly weak. It did not reach the dark waters below, lapping against an old, rusted ferryboat docked in a forgotten corner of an abandoned shipyard. It barely reached past the edge of the balcony on which its keeper stood. But the crystal sphere of magmalight, perched on a tall wooden staff, was bright enough to alert those who knew where to look.

I think so . . .

The light's keeper stood still, shrouded in a hooded black robe, staring straight ahead with a single, pupilless white eye. It didn't see the giant cargo ships slipping by on the water, nor the glow of sleepy houses on the far shore.

I don't know about this. . . .

What the eye of the Reader did see was the matrix

of forces intersecting from many worlds, specifically the force signatures of beings that might not be visible to normal sight.

Dean, just trust me.

Okay.

There was little for the Reader to see tonight. Other than the shimmering spirit of a dead bird fluttering aimlessly in the wind, the night appeared empty. All the guests were inside. Now it was a matter of keeping unwanted presences out.

Hello, a voice suddenly spoke in its head.

The Reader started, confused, sensing a strange presence in its mind — something living, a girl? But wait, it also felt like a demon. . . .

Cecitethhhh . . . The voice hissed, and the Reader's mind clouded, losing track of the forces around it. Blinded, the creature panicked, staggering —

Then the feeling was gone. The Reader's lidless eye, which had momentarily dimmed, began glowing brightly again, and its view of the forces returned. There was the still, dark night, the spirit of the dead bird. . . . The Reader sighed. His eighth-millennium birthday was approaching. Age did funny things to the senses.

✦

Meanwhile, behind the Reader, two shadowy figures hurried down a dark metal hallway undetected, into the bowels of the ferry.

We're in, Oliver thought.

Great, Emalie said in his mind, and then popped into sight between him and Dean.

"Nice work," said Oliver.

"Thanks," Emalie replied, but then she stumbled and crashed to her knees. The sound reverberated up and down the hall. Oliver glanced worriedly back toward the Reader, but it didn't turn. It had no sense of sound.

Dean knelt and helped Emalie up. "I knew this was a bad idea."

"I'm fine." Emalie shook him free. She looked pale. Oliver noticed that her eyes had changed, as they did when she made contact with demons, her pupils turning white and her irises red. "Stop looking at me like that," Emalie snapped at Oliver. "I can handle it."

"If you say so," said Oliver. He knew better than to argue with her. Still, things like this had happened to Emalie before, and they were only getting more frequent. It wasn't supposed to be possible for a human, even an Orani, to speak with the dead the way that Emalie could.

They entered the cabin of the ship. Rows of seats were bent at odd angles, strung together with cobwebs. The boat had been out of use for decades, and looked it, which was the point. No one would expect a meeting of such importance to be held here.

"This way." Oliver pushed open a door into the kitchen. The steel appliances and cabinets were covered with graffiti, the counters littered with trash.

They reached another door and Oliver paused. He could hear the echoing voices on the other side. He turned and shot a severe glance at Emalie and Dean.

"We know," Dean moaned, "stay quiet and don't get found out and all that."

"Pretty much," Oliver agreed.

"I just wish I could go." Dean pouted.

"I tried, Dean," Emalie said sympathetically.

"I know, I know. No way to make a lowly zombie invisible." Dean rolled his eyes. "It's safer anyway," he said, fingering the smooth black pendant around his neck. "Just in case . . ."

"Right," said Oliver. As far as they knew, the hindrian charm Dean was wearing had been keeping him safe from his master's orders. Emalie had found an enchantment to power up the charm, and Dean had shown no signs of being under Lythia's command, but there was still a danger. The charm was only supposed to be temporary.

"We'll tell you everything," Emalie promised.

"Have a great time," Dean grunted with a wave of his hand. "I'll be here keeping watch."

Emalie nodded and vanished again.

Oliver spectralized, disappearing as well. Then he pushed open the door and stepped through. There was no floor on the other side. He concentrated, steadying himself against the forces, and slid onto a curved, metal wall.

You there? Oliver thought to Emalie.

Right beside you, Emalie thought back. She had been able to speak in his mind since the summer. It was convenient for situations like this, but it also meant that Emalie could hear Oliver's thoughts whenever she wanted. That had taken some getting used to.

Wow, Emalie said in awe.

Thirty feet below them, at the base of sheer metal walls, were three rings of chairs. Behind them, windows looked out into black water beneath the ferry. Magmalight globes swirled white-hot between the windows.

Every chair except for two was filled by a finely dressed vampire. All eyes faced center, to the circle of space occupied by two figures: Phlox and Sebastian. They stood beside each other, shoulders touching. Oliver tensed at seeing his parents. He could almost feel the dark emotions coming off them.

"Is there anything else you can tell us?" asked Tyrus McKnight, one of Sebastian's coworkers sitting in the surrounding crowd.

"I think we've explained quite enough," Phlox replied indignantly. "We know nothing of what Bane was up to. He is —" her voice hitched, and her eyes began to glow turquoise, "— *was* his own demon."

Oliver felt a knot pulling tight in his stomach. This was the first reaction he'd seen from his parents about losing their older son. It had been two weeks since that night, when Oliver had returned home, stood in the living room, and delivered the news: "Bane's gone." He'd braced for his parents' reaction, expecting them to explode in rage, calling for vengeance against Lythia, Désirée, and even Half-Light.

But Phlox and Sebastian had barely moved. They'd been exhausted at the time, having spent many nights searching for Bane, not knowing until it was too late that Half-Light had been framing him for a series of human murders. Oliver's awful news had only seemed to press them further into the couch.

Since then, Oliver had waited nervously. Maybe their reaction would come the next evening, or the next. But the nights kept passing. Silent, tense, *empty*. Until now.

"There, there, Phloxiana," a thin voice said below. It was Mr. Ravonovich, head of Half-Light, a wiry old vampire with ancient eyes, pure white skin, and razor-sharp, parchment-colored teeth. "These are certainly unfortunate events."

"Why don't you tell *us* what Bane was up to?" asked Sebastian, his voice quiet, dangerous. "You're the ones who planned to slay him."

"What *we* planned to do, Sebastian," Ravonovich replied icily, "was whatever was necessary to protect the prophecy. We are here tonight to determine what *you* knew, not the other way around. And based on all the testimony, I think we can conclude that you were not aiding your son in his traitorous actions, which is fortunate." Ravonovich raised his voice to address the chamber. "The case of Bane Nocturne is closed, and now we must turn our attention to the future. We have only a week before the Darkling Ball, and we must ensure that nothing jeopardizes the Anointment."

Is that about you? Emalie thought.

I think so. Oliver figured that the "Anointment" was the ritual in which he would be given mystical power by the demon Vyette, power that would allow him to journey to Nexia. She would be summoned from a higher world using the Artifact.

It didn't surprise Oliver that he hadn't known the ritual's proper title. He knew almost nothing about the procedure itself, and even less about what it meant. What kind of power was he even getting? How did one travel to Nexia? All he knew was that this power was critical to him making the journey and receiving his demon, Illisius. And to opening the Gate and freeing the vampires, which would also destroy the world and everything in it, including his friends.

"Once the Anointment is completed," Ravonovich continued, "there can be no stopping us. The prophecy can no longer be tampered with, and the Gate *will* be opened."

"But what of Bane's traitorous labors?" asked Leah from the crowd.

"What Bane has done must be undone. His treachery must be found, and destroyed."

What are they talking about? Emalie asked.

Not sure, Oliver replied, but he felt an ache inside as he remembered the moment when he'd discovered that Bane had been made to fulfill the prophecy just like Oliver had. Unlike all other vampire children, who were created in a lab, Oliver and Bane had been sired from human infants.

Bane's "treachery" must have been his attempt to free Oliver from the prophecy. In that case, Oliver would need to be very careful, because just the other night he had finally discovered a false back on one of Bane's dresser drawers, and found two very secret and myste-rious objects within. Oliver didn't know yet what they did, but he was certain they were the objects Bane had planned to show him.

Yasmin spoke up from the crowd. "Is there any word on the Brotherhood of the Fallen?"

"There have been only rumors since Valentine's Day," said Malcolm LeRoux from the seat beside Ravonovich. "But we cannot be content to believe that they will let the Anointment pass without some attempt to thwart it." The Brotherhood had attacked the Darkling Ball on the night of Bane's Anointment — which ruined Bane's chance to fulfill the prophecy and passed it on to Oliver.

"Do we have any new plans this time, to avoid getting blown up?" Leah asked.

"We have hired Pyreth Guardians for the event," said Ravonovich. A murmur passed through the crowd. "And moved the ceremony's location underground."

"And what of the Rogue?" someone asked over the din. "Even the Pyreth are no match for her."

The room quieted.

"Yes," Ravonovich muttered, "the Rogue. We shall continue to be vigilant, to determine her motive. As we all know, that's all we can do for now."

Désirée? Emalie wondered.

Sounds like it, Oliver agreed. Dead Désirée was the only being powerful enough to earn that kind of respect — and perhaps some fear? — from Half-Light. And no one knew what kind of being she really was.

"And what about the boy?" Malcolm asked, his voice dripping with distaste.

"Oliver should be treated normally, to ensure a smooth path to his destiny," said Ravonovich.

"Normally?" Malcolm sneered. "We treated his traitorous brother normally and look where that got us. If you ask me, we should lock up young Oliver until the Anointment."

"We're not asking you," said Tyrus.

"So what, we're just going to let him cavort about with humans and zombies and wraiths?" Malcolm rose to his feet. "Generations will be doomed to this prison if we do not open the Gate. You're putting legions of *vampyr* at risk!"

"And you're not?" Phlox growled. "Where is your little princess? Talk about letting one cavort irresponsibly —"

"Watch your tongue," Malcolm hissed. "My daughter . . . how did you put it? Lythia is her *own* demon. I don't know where she is, or what she is up to, but I do know she is no failure like your first, and no sniveling coward like your second."

Oliver shook with anger.

Let it go, Emalie warned. He knew she was right, but still, it was taking all of his focus to remain invisible, listening to this.

Below, Phlox wasn't able to restrain herself. "Tsss —" She lunged toward Malcolm. Sebastian grabbed her by the shoulders, holding her back.

"Enough!" Ravonovich's voice boomed through the chamber. "Sit down, Malcolm. Your daughter is a traitor to the cause and has formed dangerous alliances. If I were you, I'd be rooting for young Lythia to keep out of sight until after the Anointment. If she tries again to interfere with our plans, not even your valuable research into the Artifact, or your significant sacrifices to the cause, will save you both from the ash can."

Malcolm sat, seething.

"Sebastian, Phloxiana," Ravonovich continued, "the Consortium understands that you have sacrificed much, and this will not be forgotten. Rest assured, we will be vigilantly watching out for you and Oliver in these final days."

Oliver thought that sounded more like a threat than a reassurance. Phlox felt the same way. "Meaning you don't trust us," she muttered.

"Trust is irrelevant," Ravonovich replied. "This is the end game. The final act of a drama that has graced this stage since the binding stitches of the universe were completed. Soon, the *vampyr* and the Architects will read their final lines. And if we are right, as we know we are, then we shall prevail and be free, finally free, from the shackles of Finity, and the Eternal Tomb will be destroyed."

A great chorus of earsplitting hissing engulfed the room.

Finity? What's that? Emalie asked.

Oliver had only heard the word Finity once before,

from Bane, in the moments before he was slain. *Bane said that Finity was the whole point*, he replied.

The whole point of what?

Not sure.

And what are the Architects? Emalie asked.

Origin beings, Oliver explained. *They built the universe, and the Gate.*

"Thank you all for coming," said Ravonovich. The vampires stood and gathered their coats. Oliver watched his parents shuffle from the center of the floor. No one spoke to them as they left.

Come on, said Emalie. Oliver felt her slide back through the door. He turned and did the same.

"How'd it go?" Dean asked as they left the kitchen.

"It went," said Oliver, leading the way to a broken window. He scaled down the hull of the ship to the abandoned dock. Dean jumped down, landing awkwardly on the buckled boards. Emalie reappeared beside them. They hurried away from the pier, under a looming highway overpass, and up steep lengths of stairs into the lonely city streets.

"So, did they know what Bane was up to?" Dean asked.

"I think Half-Light did, but they didn't say what," said Oliver.

"And what about Lythia?" Dean asked. "Any news?"

"No," Emalie answered, "but they're worried about her. Désirée, too. They called her the Rogue. And it sounded like they don't know what to do about her, either."

"That makes two of us," said Dean. They had been to the Underground twice in the last two weeks so that Emalie could get supplies. Both times they had passed Désirée's shop, and both times it had been closed.

"Half-Light said they'd be watching me," said Oliver. "And they're looking for Bane's treachery, whatever that is."

"The objects you found?" Dean asked.

Oliver shrugged. "And they said that once the Anointment is completed, there's no way to undo the prophecy."

"So we need to check those objects," said Emalie. "Maybe I should stop working on the Portal enchantment until we can —"

"No," said Oliver. The Portal would take Oliver, Emalie, and Dean back to the night of Oliver's death. The night that Phlox and Sebastian sired him and killed his parents. Except that maybe, just maybe, Oliver's parents hadn't been killed. Their graves had been full of pig bones. And Oliver had been told by the leader of the Brotherhood, Braiden Lang, that they were alive.

"Okay. Well, let's meet tomorrow at my place," said

Dean. When Emalie wasn't looking, he winked at Oliver. They had something else planned for tomorrow night as well. "I gotta go meet Autumn at the sewer clubs. See you guys later."

Oliver and Emalie walked quietly through the city. Oliver felt like walls were closing in. His destiny was mere days away, and he had no idea how to stop it.

CHAPTER 2

New Ashes, Old Answers

The next night, Oliver awoke to a terrible racket. His eyes snapped open and he was surprised to realize that he'd actually been sleeping. His portable video game player lay on his chest, still pulsing with tinny music and lights, muffled by his sleeping soil. He flicked it off and listened for whatever had woken him.

Crrrrackk!

The sound was violent and close by. Oliver flicked a handle and the lid of his coffin yawned open. He sat up to find Phlox on the other side of the crypt. Sebastian stood nearby, head down, hands clasped behind his back.

"Good morning, Oliver," Phlox said, her tone businesslike. She was well-dressed in a sharp black blazer, a high-collared white shirt, and black pants. Her long platinum hair was pulled back and fastened with two sticks, yet one wild strand had sprung free and dangled in front of her face.

"Hey, Mom," said Oliver. "What's up?"

"Oh," sighed Phlox, "just catching up on a little housecleaning." With that, she raised an enormous sledgehammer and slammed it down —

On Bane's coffin.

The wood exploded as the heavy stone head crashed into it. Splinters sprayed across the room. Phlox lifted the sledgehammer and struck again. The coffin lid imploded and a geyser of sleeping soil burst into the air. The sound rattled off the stone walls of the crypt.

"There we go," said Phlox, another strand of hair coming free. Oliver noted the tight purse of her mouth, the turquoise glow in her eyes, the fierce *v* shape of her brow. . . .

Crrrraaackk!

"Nice work, honey," Sebastian said supportively. His eyes had begun to glow with emotion as well, his face similarly tense.

Phlox's next swing crashed through the bottom of the bed and into the dresser drawers below. The sledgehammer came away wrapped in ratty black T-shirts and torn jeans. Phlox shook the clothes free, then threw down the hammer again.

Oliver watched his brother's coffin splinter apart, collapsing into a pile of broken wood and clothes and soil, and felt his face grow tight as well.

Finally, this was good-bye.

The sledgehammer head clanged to the stone floor. Phlox turned to Sebastian. "Would you like a turn?" she asked solemnly.

Sebastian looked down at his hands. His left, though almost fully regrown, was still slightly smaller than the right, and a ghostly white. Sebastian was finally able to do most of the normal things that an adult vampire could do, but he shook his head. "You can finish."

"Oliver?" Phlox asked, holding the sledgehammer toward him.

"You do it," said Oliver quietly.

"All right, then." Phlox swung ferociously, crushing the pile of remains and even cracking the floor in the process.

Oliver was relieved to finally see his parents releasing their emotions, and also that he'd gotten Bane's hidden objects out of the coffin just in time.

Phlox stopped again, this time letting the hammer fall from her hand and clatter to the floor. She stared hard at the wreckage, her eyes burning. "Shall we?" she whispered.

"Of course," said Sebastian. He gathered armfuls of the tangled wood and clothing. "Oliver, would you like to help?"

"Yeah." Oliver slipped out of bed and filled his arms as well. He followed Sebastian upstairs. Within his load was one of Bane's leather jackets, which still carried a faint scent of Bane's many noxious colognes. The smell made Oliver's gut clench. He never imagined that he could have missed his annoying brother this much. Then again, until the moment before Bane was slain, Oliver had had no idea how similar they were. It was so unfair.

Phlox followed Oliver as they climbed to the surface floor of the house. They slipped through the steel door, around the broken refrigerator, and carried the remains across the dilapidated space, through a huge hole in the far wall, stopping at a giant stone fireplace. Rain fell gently into the room from rotted holes above.

Sebastian tossed his armful inside. Oliver did the same. Phlox followed, then pulled a tiny glass jar from her pocket and hurled it at the pile. The jar exploded and a thick pink substance splattered onto the remains. It was jellied magma, which aided in starting forges and fires and getting them to burn far hotter than a conventional oven or flame ever could.

Sebastian struck a match and tossed it in. There was a great sucking gasp of air, and Bane's things burst into white-hot flames.

Oliver squinted at the blaze, but forced himself not to look away. Phlox and Sebastian stood on either side of him, doing the same. Bane's clothes and boots began to melt. The wood blackened and crumbled in the searing heat.

"*Cindrethth* . . ." Phlox whispered slowly. It was an ancient Skrit word for a slain vampire, meaning "returned to ash."

As his vision was slowly blinded by green, Oliver saw Bane's face in his mind, that night in the overgrown cemetery, the last moment of his existence. His look of shock as he'd turned to dust — a look that Oliver had never seen from his brother before. That gut-clenching feeling increased, and Oliver longed to —

Admit it, he said to himself. Yes, he wanted to cry again, as he had that night with help from the apparition. He wanted that painful feeling that strangely seemed to make things better. But he couldn't do it alone. Different as he was, he was still a vampire. And he hadn't seen the apparition at all in the weeks since.

Oliver felt a hand, and turned to find Phlox taking his. She squeezed it so tightly that Oliver's finger bones came close to snapping. "This won't happen again," she whispered.

"We won't let it," Sebastian agreed softly.

The fire cooled and soon died. All that remained was a pile of ash and cinders.

"Time for breakfast," Phlox said quietly, and turned away. Sebastian followed.

Oliver gazed at the ashes for another moment, then joined them.

In the kitchen, Phlox threw herself into making a

fresh blood angel cake, Bane's favorite. Oliver sat at the island, in his usual place. Sebastian stood by the counter. Bane's old seat remained empty.

Oliver found that he was nervous. The feeling grew, and he was three bites into his cake before he figured out why.

It was time.

He'd been waiting, trying to understand how his parents truly felt about losing Bane. Now that he'd seen it — felt it — he could say what he'd been holding inside.

"Guys," Oliver began, "I know."

Phlox stopped working at the counter, but didn't turn around yet. "What's that, honey?" Oliver was certain she'd heard him. Sebastian put down his goblet.

"I know about Bane and the prophecy," he continued. Phlox gazed at him blankly. Oliver felt the urge to shut up and get out of the room, but he pressed on. "I know all of it. Bane was sired, like me. He was the first try at the prophecy, but it didn't work."

Oliver watched Phlox's face darken. She had lied to him about this, telling him that Bane had been born like a normal vampire child.

"Yes, Ollie," said Sebastian. "Bane told you, I take it?"

"Yeah." Oliver didn't feel any better for saying this. "Why didn't *you* tell me?"

Phlox gazed at the floor, shaking her head. It was a

look of disappointment that Oliver had only seen in the last few months. "Not telling you about Bane, or about your destiny to begin with . . . it was all to give you a better chance at a normal childhood."

"But it hasn't been normal."

"Well," said Sebastian, "we thought it could be, at least until it was time for you to fulfill the prophecy. That was our mistake. Still, it's almost over. Once you're Anointed, things will be better, until the day when Illisius comes to you." Sebastian smiled. "And then we'll be free."

"But . . ." Oliver felt a sharp stab of worry. The very things his dad — that all the New World vampires — looked forward to was something Oliver didn't want. "What if what happened to Bane happens to me?"

"Ollie," said Sebastian, "we won't let anyone slay you."

"No, not that," Oliver said, struggling to get these thoughts out. "I mean, failing at the prophecy, getting left out. Bane said he never felt right after his Anointment failed."

Phlox moved around the island and put an arm across Oliver's shoulders. "Honey, we made our mistakes with Bane. . . . But it's different with you."

"Bane never had the annual force treatments from Dr. Vincent," Sebastian added. "And we're summoning Vyette much sooner for you than we did for him."

Oliver nodded, but inside, his fears weren't subsiding. This wasn't the way he'd hoped the conversation would go. *What did I expect?* he wondered. But that was easy. Having finally glimpsed his parents' emotions about Bane... *I hoped they might be so upset that they'd hear me out when I said...*

"But maybe we'd be better off if I didn't have the prophecy at all."

Phlox and Sebastian exchanged a look. "What do you mean?" Phlox asked.

"Well, I mean, that would make all this go away, wouldn't it?" reasoned Oliver. "We don't know if the prophecy is going to work, but if I didn't have it at all, then we could be normal." Neither parent replied. Oliver didn't know what else to do except keep talking. "It's like what Grandma said," he continued, echoing what Bane had said to him. Phlox sighed at the mention of her mother, but Oliver went on. "Maybe Earth isn't so bad."

"Oliver," said Sebastian, "first of all, your grandmother and the rest of the Old World have never embraced modern studies enough to fully grasp that Earth is a prison. The blood and chaos are seductive, but those are just the trappings of Finity."

"What's Finity?" Oliver asked.

"Finity is time with an end," Sebastian explained. "It is a limitation of worlds made of matter. Nowhere in the universe is Finity stronger than on Earth. Life, death, and all the desperation and emotion they create, it's all due to Finity. You can see it played out in the human comedy, with their love and wars, their shortsightedness, their lack of awareness. It's all because of their short lives. Demons weren't meant for such a fate."

Oliver thought about this. "That's why you call Earth the Eternal Tomb."

"Hah." Sebastian smiled. "It's been called that, yes. When a *vampyr* demon is sent here, there is no escape. The end will come, compliments of Finity, whether by a stake or sunlight or the effects of time. . . . Which is, of course, why we yearn to be free, why we will be."

Oliver hesitated, but then, as he'd been practicing over this long year, said what was on his mind. "Bane said that Finity was a good thing."

Sebastian and Phlox shared another look, and Oliver felt a surge of that old frustration. They still knew things that he didn't. "Why are you looking at each other like that?"

Sebastian looked quizzically at Oliver. "Do *you* feel that way?"

"I don't know what to feel," said Oliver honestly. "I just wish we could be normal. Bane thought that if we undid the prophecy, then —"

"Listen," Sebastian said sternly, "things *can* be normal. Once we're free. But undoing the prophecy is unthinkable."

"Come on, Dad. Why? Bane thought that —"

"Bane is gone," said Phlox.

Oliver felt the weight of those words settle over the three of them. He looked at his parents' weary faces, and couldn't think of anything else to say. They had lost a son, and were doing what they thought was best to protect Oliver. He got that. And they believed in the prophecy, and freedom for the *vampyr*. He got that, too.

But what about what I feel? Oliver thought desperately. He had to keep trying to make them understand. "What about my friends?" he asked. *What about my human parents?* he thought inside. "Opening the Gate will destroy them —"

"We've been very understanding of your friendships," Phlox said carefully, "but you have to understand that such things, they — they're just not possible. I know it's hard but you're just going to have to —"

"Get over it?" Oliver muttered, echoing his mom's words from the winter.

Phlox's eyes smoldered. "Oliver, we're trying to do what's best for you."

"But maybe what's best for me is undoing the prophecy —"

"*Then what?*" Sebastian suddenly roared, and hurled his goblet across the room. It clanged from the wall to the counter to the floor. "Even if it were true,

Oliver . . . even if undoing the prophecy *were* best for all of us, it wouldn't matter. Do you have any idea what Half-Light will do if we defy them? We wouldn't even have you if it weren't for Half-Light, and we will not lose you because of some misplaced feelings or friendships. We won't discuss this further."

"You have to see it from our perspective," added Phlox, her tone still gentle. "There's no alternative to fulfilling your prophecy. If there's anything to be learned from what happened to Bane . . . that's it."

Oliver wanted to argue further, but once again, he understood what Phlox and Sebastian were saying. Half-Light would likely slay the whole family before allowing the prophecy to be undone. So really, did his parents even have a choice about any of this? Maybe they didn't.

"Fine," Oliver said quietly. He slid away from the counter and headed for the stairs.

"Oliver, we mean it," Sebastian said behind him.

"I know."

Oliver dressed for school, grabbed Bane's secret items, and left through the sewer. His parents might not have a choice, but he did. And if there was one thing that *he* had learned from his brother, it was to do his own thing.

CHAPTER 3

The Firefly and the Message

Oliver was one of the first to arrive at school. He leaped onto one of the basketball hoops and sat on the rim. A couple younger kids were cornering a cat in the far corner of the playground. The sky was heavy with low clouds, tinted orange by the city lights. A cool breeze blew, and it smelled like rain.

Oliver removed Bane's objects from his sweatshirt pocket: a felt bag and a small scroll tied with yarn. He put the scroll back in his pocket, loosened the bag's silk drawstring, and gently emptied the contents into his palm.

You won't believe what I did, bro, Bane had said just before he was slain. In Oliver's hand was a tiny box wrapped in a strip of paper. He unwrapped the paper. On it was a short message, in handwriting he didn't recognize:

For Oliver.

The box was carved from pure amethyst, its top and bottom connected with a gold hinge. Oliver slowly opened it. Inside was a small pillow of black felt. On it lay a single firefly. It didn't move. It looked dead, but it might also be in some frozen state, waiting to be awakened.

"Hello?" Oliver murmured at the insect. "I'm here." The firefly didn't stir.

Bane had said that he'd spoken to Selene. That she'd told him how to undo Oliver's prophecy and that whatever he'd been doing was almost ready. *Bane, what were you up to?* This firefly must have been part of Selene. Maybe it contained a bit of her life force.

"Hey," he said to the firefly.

"Who are you talking to, Nocturne?"

Oliver snapped the box closed and looked down to see his classmate Theo standing at the base of the basketball hoop. "Nobody," said Oliver coldly, slipping the box back into his pocket.

"That sounds about right," Theo remarked. He looked around the empty playground, his hands in his pockets.

Oliver braced for what Theo would say next. They had never been friends, but since the night of Bane's slaying, when Oliver had ruined a game of Gargoyle Tag by attacking Theo's friend Maggots in a fit of rage, Theo had been colder than ever. Oliver felt like a timer was ticking. Every night, he expected some kind of revenge for that outburst. And the longer he had to wait, the more worried he became that the payback was going to be brutal.

But Theo just stood there. After a few seconds, Oliver finally snapped: "What?"

Theo glared up at him, but then looked away again. "Heard about your brother," he said.

"Yeah, so?"

"So . . ." Theo began, and lunged up into the air. Oliver flinched, but Theo grabbed the backboard and swung himself onto it, sitting above Oliver's shoulder. Strangely, he used only one hand. The other stayed in his pocket. "That sucks, that's what. Even for you."

Oliver scowled. "Yeah, well, why do you care?"

"I don't, really." Theo stared out across the playground. "But if you're wondering why you got off after what you did to Maggots, that's why."

"So what, I'm, like, lucky?"

"Nah, you're just not broken in ten places, like you shoulda been, after what you did."

"Okay," said Oliver. Theo kept sitting there. Oliver was confused. "And?"

"My sister was torched," said Theo. Torched was another term for being slain. "She was wild, so she had it coming, but still . . ." Theo's eyes glowed with a tinge of deep blue.

"Huh," Oliver offered.

"My dad took it pretty hard," Theo said quietly. "He wanted revenge, but they never found out who did it."

"That's too bad," Oliver said sincerely, yet with a note of distrust.

Theo pulled his other hand from his pocket and made a show of flexing it. A few of his fingers were purple and broken. Theo had shown up at school with injuries before. No one ever talked about them, but it was known that sometimes Theo's dad could get very angry, even for a vampire. "You gotta get some vengeance," Theo said, and his voice lowered. "Otherwise, you do other things."

Oliver waited for Theo to continue, but he didn't. "Okay," Oliver finally said. "Thanks."

"Hey, Theo!" Maggots, Suzyn, and Kym were strolling across the playground. "What are you doing?"

"Oh," said Theo. "Back to business. Hey, guys!" he shouted, then turned and shoved Oliver violently off the hoop. As Oliver tumbled to the pavement, Theo soared over to his friends and they shared a good laugh. Theo sauntered away, an arm around Kym, but with his damaged hand still hidden in his pocket.

Oliver dragged himself to his feet. More kids were arriving now, filling up the playground. He felt the objects in his pocket, frustrated that he would have to wait to decipher them further.

Oliver headed inside early, brushing absently through the students who were milling around by the door, joking and playing. Theo's words had him distracted. Vengeance. He thought of Lythia, and imagined lunging at her, plunging a stake through her heart and watching her dissolve to ash . . . and he found that he very much wanted that. It made his teeth grit, his fists clench. *There you go, bro*, he could imagine his brother saying approvingly.

He knocked at the back door, but there was no answer. Trying the handle, he found the door open. The halls were alive with glowing grotesqua. Oliver proceeded upstairs, past the silent, leering demon faces and swirling battle scenes.

Rodrigo, a vampire who secretly worked as the school's night janitor, stood by Oliver's classroom door. His hands were coated in shimmering neon. He waved them around, sculpting a new grotesqua image, mumbling to himself in Skrit as he did so. Colors dripped from his fingers, composing images.

The scene showed a hall full of vampires dancing, dressed in fine tuxedos and gowns. To one side, an orchestra played, their bows waving in unison. The dancers twirled. Balconies arced above, and at the height of the scene, a glowing moon shone down. The Darkling Ball.

The room reminded Oliver of the one he'd visited in Bane's memory. After its destruction, Half-Light's main offices and the ballroom had been moved into the top floors of the Iniquity Bank Tower, a tall black skyscraper downtown. Oliver had never been to the ball, but of course he would be there this year. So would the rest of his class — this was the first year that they were old enough to attend.

"Looks great, Rodrigo."

"Thank you, sir. I love the music," said Rodrigo wistfully, as if he could hear it now.

"Me, too," said Oliver truthfully. In honor of Waning Sun, the full *Melancholia* was being performed. Since the entire piece was over two months long, the performance had begun weeks ago, and would culminate Friday night at the Darkling Ball, with the unveiling of the newest movement. Oliver was actually looking forward to hearing it, especially since he played cello himself.

"It will certainly be a grand night," said Rodrigo.

"Yeah," Oliver replied quietly. Rodrigo didn't know the half of it. Oliver wondered what he would think, what everyone at school would think if they knew about Oliver's prophecy, and about the Anointment. Only members of Half-Light knew of Oliver's destiny. Would his classmates, teachers, Rodrigo even, think differently of him? Would it make him a celebrity again, as he'd briefly been last winter, when everyone thought he'd only befriended Emalie in order to torment her by killing her cousin? It would make things even harder, Oliver guessed. He already felt guilty enough about wanting to undo the prophecy.

Oliver entered his classroom. He was the first to arrive in the candlelit room, and went immediately to his desk. As he sat down, he caught a familiar scent, felt a twinge of excitement, and reached under the desk. Sure enough, something was wedged between the desktop and the metal bar.

It was a key chain: an empty ring attached to a tiny black plastic square. There was a curved space at the top of the square that revealed the edge of something inside, made of clear plastic. He pinched and pulled, revealing a small magnifying glass.

Leaning over, Oliver held the glass over the desk, close to the wood surface. The spot he was focusing on was blank, but changed when Oliver whispered: "*Segretthh . . .*" a Skrit word meaning "secret."

Charred lines appeared in the desktop, making words so tiny that the magnifying glass was necessary for reading them. Emalie had created this device as a safer way of passing notes than regular paper. Only Oliver or

Emalie's voice could activate the message. What Oliver read now caused a ripple of worried excitement:

it's ready. meet at Dean's. 4 A.M.

It was the Portal. Finally, he would find out for sure if his parents were alive. *And then what?* Oliver thought. *Am I really going to go find them? What good will that do?* He had no idea. All he knew was that if they were alive out there somewhere, he desperately wanted to know them, and well, that was that.

Oliver blew on the words and they disappeared in a small cloud of ash.

Moments later, the rest of his class began piling into the room. Theo and his friends immediately leaped up to the ceiling, where they formed their upside-down circle to joke and flirt and make fun of the others entering, like Berthold and Carly. Even Seth took some abuse, Maggots making a joke about his hair even though it was the exact same curly blond that it had been for years. No jokes came Oliver's way, thanks to Theo, he guessed, and so he settled back into his seat and waited for the long school night to be over.

CHAPTER 4

A Day Older . . . And Farther Away

As Oliver left school that evening, he paused. Sometimes he still expected Bane to be skulking outside, waiting to walk home with him and harass him along the way. He felt a fresh wave of anger, toward Lythia and Désirée, toward Half-Light. . . . But these thoughts would have to wait, because tonight, there was something else important to be done.

After a quick stop along the way, Oliver arrived at Dean's house just before four. He found two people on the porch. One was Emalie's great-aunt Kathleen, whom Oliver had recently met. She was a middle-aged, heavyset woman, an Orani like Emalie, and helped her with learning enchantments and skills. "Hi, Oliver," she said as he climbed the steps.

"Hey."

Beside her was a man with dark straight hair in a youthful mop on his head, his hands in the pockets of his black leather jacket. His eyes had a familiar shape and darkness.

"Mr. Watkins?" Oliver asked.

Emalie's father, Cole, looked down at Oliver apprehensively. "So you're Oliver."

Oliver nodded. While he'd been in Emalie's house many times, this was the first time that they'd ever met. "Nice to meet you," said Oliver. With the way that Cole was looking at him, like he was someone not to be trusted, Oliver didn't bother with the human custom of sticking out his hand.

But then Cole did. Oliver shook it.

"I know," said Cole, "that as a father I should probably . . . well . . . probably *something*. But I don't know what. You're Emalie's best friend. Nothing I can do about that, is there?"

Best friend? Oliver felt a rush, but managed to just shrug. "Guess not. I'm not dangerous —"

"Yes you are," Cole said quickly. "But so is the world Emalie's a part of now. That her mom was part of." A slight frost edged Cole's words. "So just don't pretend that you're not, and we'll be fine."

"Sure," said Oliver. He thought that was a pretty good perspective to have on things.

Dean opened the door. "Hey, everybody." He craned his neck out, gazing up and down the street. "Come on in," he said.

They followed Dean through the dark living room to the kitchen, which was lit by a candle chandelier and bustling with activity.

"Hey, Uncle Cole," Dean's younger brother, Kyle, said breathlessly, racing past. "Oliver, Oliver, Oliver!" he shouted, jumping up and down. He was in his pajamas, his hair sticking this way and that. "Check it out!" He held up a small plastic figurine that was missing one arm and both its legs. Kyle grabbed the remaining arm and yanked it free.

There was a sharp popping sound. "Oh, no, my arm!" The doll moaned in a high-pitched electronic voice.

"Ha!" Kyle shouted. "So great!"

Oliver nodded. Dismemberment dolls were popular with vampire kids and teens. Even just pretending to tear someone's limbs off helped them work out their frustrations. Dean had gotten this one for Kyle in the Underground.

"Knock it off, Kyle," said his older sister, Elizabeth, who sat on a stool at the kitchen counter. She was also still in her pajamas, and was busily making sushi rolls, her nose wrinkled in disgust.

Oliver could smell why: Though the large plate beside her held a wonderful display of different maki rolls and sushi featuring tuna, salmon, avocado, and crabmeat, Elizabeth was now doing the rolls with more zombie-appropriate items inside. She winced, sinking her fingers into a small bowl of light pink meat with a squishing sound.

"Hi, Elizabeth," said Oliver meekly.

"Hey," she replied without looking up. It had been a few months since Oliver, Emalie, and Dean had needed to draw Elizabeth's blood to perform the master location spell, but Elizabeth hadn't exactly warmed up to Oliver yet, or to Dean, for that matter.

"Looking good, honey!" Dean's mom, Tammy, popped up from behind the counter, holding a large chocolate cake on a glass plate. "Hey, brother," she said to Cole in her usual half-out-of-breath way, giving him a quick, one-armed hug. "Hi, Oliver." She slid the cake down on the table. "Boy, it's been so long since I've made a normal cake. I almost forgot how!" Tammy looked over at Dean and smiled. "Just good old-fashioned sugar, flour, and butter."

Dean smiled back. "Sounds boring," he quipped. Oliver watched the interaction, and felt glad for it. Dean being undead was still hard on everyone, but there were moments, like right now, when it seemed to be going fine.

Tammy checked her watch. "Now, if Mitch would just get here —"

"Got 'em!" Mitch popped into the kitchen, holding a small box of birthday candles and removing a yellow hard hat as he did so. Mitch had once worked for an

Internet company as a programmer. Now, in order to be on a nocturnal schedule with Dean, he was a night technician installing fiber-optic lines beneath the city.

"How was work, Dad?" Dean asked.

"Hah, funny night," said Mitch, shaking his head. "Alvarez and I were putting in lines under Denny Way, and we ran into a cranky zombie pod by the new Whole Foods." Mitch popped open the fridge and grabbed a beer.

"Was everything all right?" Tammy asked, pausing in her candle placing to give Mitch a concerned look. She still worried about his new line of work.

"Fine, honey, fine," said Mitch with a smile. "Alvarez didn't get what was going on, as usual. He still thinks the zombies are homeless people." Mitch rolled his eyes. "Anyway, once the pod calmed down, I showed them your picture, son," he said to Dean. "They wanted to know how you kept so much of your hair." He turned to Tammy. "You could go into business with zombie care, honey!"

"Mitch," Tammy said with a sigh. She began lighting the candles.

Oliver remembered the nights back in the winter, after Dean had first returned, when Mitch had been much less enthusiastic about his nocturnal life. He seemed to be enjoying it now. And Dean listened to his stories with undivided attention.

The back door burst open. Tammy glanced at the clock. "Is that —"

"Relax, Mom," said Dean, all smiles as Autumn Fitch entered the kitchen. "Hey, Autumn," he said, his voice raising ever-so-slightly in pitch.

"Hi, Dean," said Autumn. "I'm not too late, am I?"

"Oh, no, course not," Dean replied instantaneously. Oliver noticed Dean's hands doing nervous gymnastics: into his pockets, back out to drum on his sides, into his pockets again. . . .

Elizabeth huffed loudly.

"We should take our places," said Tammy, picking up the cake.

Everyone filed into the dark dining room. Tammy placed the burning cake on the table, and they all scattered around the room and into the living room beyond, finding places to hide. Oliver scrambled up to the ceiling and crouched in a corner.

A silent moment passed, then the front door clicked open. "Hey, guys?" Footsteps creaked across the living room, clopped on the kitchen tiles, padded onto the dining room carpet —

"SURPRISE!"

The lights flicked on and everyone jumped out. Emalie's face went white, her eyes wide. She threw her hands over her mouth.

"Ha-appy birthday," Tammy began, and everyone

joined in. Emalie watched, her eyes welling when she spotted her dad in the group.

After the singing, Emalie cut the cake and they ate it with ice cream. Tammy brought out a trio of red sauces in metal bowls, and was careful to explain which one was normal raspberry sauce, which one was just for Dean and Autumn, and which one was specifically for Oliver.

They sat around the living room, eating and chatting. Oliver found himself even more quiet than usual. He watched the kids and parents, and tried to imagine Phlox and Sebastian here at this party. He could only picture them standing off to the side, too well-dressed, silent. But of course, it would have been improper for vampires to even attend a human event.

But what did "proper" matter? These parents — Cole, Tammy, Mitch — had drastically changed their lives for their children, sacrificed what was proper and normal, no matter the cost. Would Phlox and Sebastian ever do the same? Cole had shaken Oliver's hand. He thought back to the one time that Phlox and Tammy had met, before the trip to Morosia. Phlox had been awful.

Watching the party around him, Oliver's thoughts darkened further. If his parents and Half-Light had their way, and Oliver fulfilled his prophecy, everything in this room would be destroyed. All that Dean's and Emalie's families had sacrificed would be for nothing.

Cole had been more right than he knew. Oliver was very dangerous. They had invited their destroyer to the party.

There was sushi and presents. The Aunders got Emalie a gift card for Glazer's, which was Emalie's favorite photo shop.

"No way," she exclaimed when she opened the box from Dean. She pulled out a long length of tailbones, shiny white and enameled. "Is it . . ." Emalie asked. Oliver knew it was an iguana tail.

"Isabella Island," said Dean, referring to the island in the Galápagos, "from the wolf volcano caldera."

"That's so cool!" Emalie exclaimed.

"Cleaned and polished the vertebrae myself," said Dean proudly.

Oliver watched with growing nerves. His gift was next.

Emalie picked up the small box, unwrapping the satin paper and horse mane bow that vampires used for wrapping, ends always expertly folded so that no tape was necessary. She held up the tiny gift box, made of thin wood, and opened the hinged lid, digging into tissue paper. Oliver heard Autumn whisper girlishly to Dean, and sank to new depths of embarrassment.

"It's . . ." Emalie pulled out a long, narrow length of fabric, holding it up in front of her. "A scarf."

"What's it do?" Kyle asked skeptically.

"Um, nothing, really," said Oliver weakly. "It's just a scarf." He didn't bother to mention that it was made of moon-spun silk from Naraka, some of the finest in the world. Moon-spun silk was also supposed to gather flattering light around the wearer.

"It's really pretty," said Emalie, smiling at him and wrapping it around her neck.

Oliver wanted to melt away. He'd looked at lots of pendants and magical charms, all kinds of important and powerful objects, but knowing that Dean had already gotten her the iguana tail, he'd wanted to do something different. Except what did you get Emalie? What did you get for the girl that you . . . well, sorta . . . *Don't think that!* he shouted to himself, in case Emalie was listening.

When he looked up, he found her smiling his way. *I really like it*, she thought to him. Oliver managed to nod.

Soon, Elizabeth and Kyle had to return to bed.

"Do we need to go, Dad?" Emalie asked Cole.

"I gave him the morning off," said Aunt Kathleen, with a wink to Emalie. She was Cole's boss, as the owner of a small fleet of salmon boats.

"I'd be worried about you not getting your sleep," said Cole, "but then I know these have been normal hours for you, lately."

Emalie smiled sheepishly. "Thanks."

Dean, Autumn, Oliver, and Emalie headed out to the tiny backyard. There was a sweet smell from the last tomatoes in the garden, and the grass was littered with the first fallen leaves. A light mist had begun to fall, and they zipped up their sweatshirts.

Dean grabbed an old basketball from the grass, and the group moved to the driveway beside the house. They split into teams, Autumn and Dean versus Emalie and Oliver.

"Pass it!" Emalie called, racing past Dean. Oliver flicked her the ball, and she immediately vanished, reappearing on the roof behind the backboard.

Dean was leaping up right behind her. Emalie laughed, dribbling across the sloped roof, Dean sidestepping to keep her from the basket.

"Oliver!" she called. Oliver got a running start past Autumn and leaped. At the same time, Emalie hooked the ball over her head. Oliver caught it in midflight as he sailed past the basket, which was down by his knees. He flicked it off the backboard, only to have it swatted away from the rim by Autumn as she arced through the air.

"Nice!" called Dean, jumping off the roof.

They played to breathless exhaustion, the zombies winning, despite Oliver and Emalie's best attempts. It was fun to watch Dean come up with new levels of awkwardness to justify bumping or falling into Autumn, and most of all, Oliver enjoyed the high fives with

Emalie — all business, no smiles; she got so competitive in games like this.

And then there was one moment, after Oliver hit a tricky shot while falling to the ground. Emalie helped him up with two hands, and Oliver lurched to his feet, and they ended up within inches of each other. For a moment their eyes locked, and Oliver swam out of balance. Her eyes were so clear, so enormous, and her face, and her skin, slightly aglow from the scarf, and the scent of her, warm and alive. Oliver felt like he was falling toward her even though he was standing still —

Ah! Emalie disappeared. Oliver felt her invisible hands push him away. She winked back into sight at the far end of the driveway, picking up the ball and checking it to Autumn, her eyes firmly *not* on Oliver.

After the game ended, Dean looked around. "Where's Emalie?"

"Don't know," said Oliver. But he sensed her nearby. "There she is," he said, pointing to the roof. Oliver started toward the side of the house.

"I'll be, um, up in a sec," said Dean, "I'm just gonna . . . er, walk Autumn out."

"Right," said Oliver, smiling. He climbed up the wall to the roof, sitting beside Emalie on the narrow peak, overlooking the sleepy neighborhood.

"Cool party, huh?" he said.

Emalie sniffled and wiped at her nose. She was wrapping and unwrapping her finger with the scarf.

"Hey, what is it?"

"I'm thirteen," she said with a heavy sigh.

Oliver wasn't sure what to say. He could see how a birthday could be a downer for a human, considering they had so few of them. "Well, now we're the same age. That's cool."

Emalie huffed. "But next year I'll be fourteen."

"Me, too."

Emalie frowned at him. "And what about when I'm fifteen?" Her eyes burned.

"Well," Oliver began, but then he understood. "I'll still be fourteen."

Emalie sighed. "And then I'll be, like, eighteen and in college and you'll still be fourteen. And then I'll be old, like, *thirty,* and you'll only be . . ."

Oliver did the math immediately. "Sixteen." His insides sank.

Emalie nodded quietly.

Oliver thought of that moment during the game, when their eyes had locked and he'd been dizzy and he'd wanted to . . .

I know, Emalie thought to him, her gaze still distant.

Oliver's head fell. Long seconds passed and he couldn't

think of anything to say. Finally he tried, "It's not for a while yet."

"But it's gonna happen," said Emalie.

"Or maybe I'll just destroy everything first."

"Don't say that. We're going to stop the prophecy, I promise."

"Okay," Oliver agreed, but he felt a shudder of fear.

I know you're scared, Emalie thought to him. *We can be scared together.*

Okay, Oliver replied, despite having a shameful thought: *Vampires aren't supposed to be scared*. But that was just a myth. Even big bad Bane had been scared, in a way.

It took a moment for Oliver to notice Emalie taking his arm and pulling it up from his side. "What —" he began, but then couldn't finish.

She laid it across her shoulders and leaned against him. Oliver felt the warmth of her against his side and felt a great, freezing rush, like all his molecules were unsticking.

Emalie put her head on his shoulder. "I wish my mom was here tonight," she said.

"Have you had any more dreams about her?" Oliver asked. Emalie had dreams where she felt like she was looking out her mother's eyes, like she was with her somewhere. Margaret had been missing for almost three years. She'd left one morning for her job as a flight attendant and hadn't returned. Over the winter, Emalie had learned that her mother was Orani like she was, and that her disappearance was no accident, but no one knew where she'd gone or why. Then, in Fortuna, the town in Italy near the Underworld city of Morosia, they'd found two more mysterious clues: There had been an ancient statue in a museum, of a woman named Phoebe who looked exactly like Emalie's mom. Then there was a photo of Margaret and the oracle Selene in a town called Arcana, from the year 1868.

"I have," said Emalie. "They've been different, though. The places she's in seem, like, modern. One time there was this shop. It almost looked like Désirée's, but different. Lately there have been these long tunnels, and tall orange lights, and it's really hot. She feels closer. And scared."

"Of what?"

"Don't know." Emalie looked up at the faint stars. "I need to find her."

"We will." Oliver tried to sound confident.

Footsteps scraped on the roof. Oliver quickly pulled his arm from Emalie's shoulder, and scooted away.

"Hey, guys." Dean plopped down beside Emalie.

"How'd it go?" Oliver asked, trying to brighten his tone. Dean's face split into a goofy grin, and though he didn't blush like a human, his purple blotches did seem to darken. Oliver smiled, too. "Well done."

"Yeah," Dean said with a sigh. He pulled a package from his pocket. "Check it, I brought some chocolate-dipped roaches." He popped one of the crunchy morsels in his mouth, then passed the bag to Oliver, who took a couple and gave it back.

Emalie intercepted the bag. "What the heck," she said. "It's my birthday." She pulled out a creature and bravely tossed it into her mouth, winced slightly at the feel of tiny legs against her tongue, then bit down. Her face puckered, but then she nodded scientifically. "Huh, that's not that bad." She kept chewing. "I'm eating bugs," she announced, swallowing the creature. Then she burst out laughing. "That's got to be a sign about my social life."

Oliver and Dean laughed, too, relief washing over the roof.

"They're actually pretty healthy," said Dean. "Raised in —"

Emalie held out her hand. "Tell me nothing. Please. Whatever you're gonna say, I know I don't want to know." She took another and started chewing. "So gross," she said around the mouthful.

They laughed some more. Oliver felt like he could *almost* forget what they'd just talked about.

"Hey," Dean was saying to Emalie, "so, the Portal is ready?"

"Oh, yeah, but actually, I left it at home," Emalie admitted. "I didn't think we'd have time . . ."

Dean's eyes went wide. "You *knew*, didn't you? About the surprise party?"

Emalie smiled sheepishly. "Kinda, yeah."

"Oh, man!"

"I can't help it!" she said, laughing. "Besides, you guys have minds like billboards when you're trying to keep a secret!"

"Great," Oliver muttered.

"We'll do it tomorrow night," she said. "My place."

"Okay," said Oliver.

"Dude," Dean said to Emalie, "that was so funny when your dad was all, *Hey, let me try the zombie sauce*. The face he made!"

Emalie laughed, shaking her head. "I don't know what he was thinking."

Oliver watched them, smiling at their laughter, but not joining them. The dark thoughts were returning. *You were made to destroy them*. There was no escaping it. He had to find a way out of his prophecy, had to find his human parents, had to find an existence of his own choosing. Oliver reached into his pocket. He hadn't shown them Bane's objects yet.

"And then you switched Kyle's California roll with the intestine surprise," Emalie added, giggling harder.

"I thought he was gonna vomit!" Dean gasped.

Oliver put away the objects and tried, as hard as he knew how, to join in the laughter. He just wanted things to be normal! To have friends and have fun and sit on a roof with nothing to worry about. Even if it would never be true, he had to try to pretend, at least for tonight.

CHAPTER 5

Selene's Last Breath

Dinners were quiet now. Oliver felt like he could hear the echoes of conversations at the table from the past, or from another world where Bane was still with them.

Charles, how was school tonight? Phlox would ask in that overly formal tone, like she was already bracing for Bane's sarcastic reply: *Whatever. Who cares.* Phlox's eyes would start to smolder, leading to a sharp comment about the importance of school. Oliver would be sitting there thinking Bane was so annoying, yet glad nobody was asking him how his night was. . . .

"How was your night, Oliver?" Phlox asked.

"Fine," Oliver mumbled over his goblet. In truth, Tuesday night at school had been nearly unbearable. Oliver had to listen to endless talk among his classmates about the Ball, which was no pleasant distraction from thinking about his recent conversation with Emalie. Worse, he'd found a note from Emalie saying she had to push back doing the Portal to Wednesday, because the final part of the preparation hadn't worked.

"Have you thought about who you'll ask to the Ball?"

Oliver kept his gaze firmly on his plate. Unbelievable. Did they really expect to just sit here and talk about the Ball like everything was normal? Like something as stupid as a date to the dance even mattered? As if the beginning of the end of the world wasn't on the schedule for that same night?

"Nope," Oliver replied stiffly. He shoveled pie into his mouth.

"I would imagine your classmates are looking forward to their first Ball," Phlox went on.

"Guess," said Oliver.

"Well, I'm sure you'll find a date in time," said Sebastian.

The doorbell chimed. Oliver saw Phlox shoot a glance at Sebastian as he got up.

"Who's that?" Oliver asked.

"We have some visitors this evening," Phlox said, looking at her plate.

Oliver heard the sewer door open, and then the sound of multiple voices and footsteps returning to the kitchen.

"Hello, Oliver." Dr. Vincent entered the room, removing a long gray coat from his broad shoulders and setting a black briefcase on the table, among their plates. Behind him, Tyrus entered, followed by Sebastian.

"Oliver," said Sebastian, "Dr. Vincent is here to give you your final force treatment for Friday."

"I don't want it," Oliver said dejectedly.

"Ah, no need to worry, Oliver," said Dr. Vincent with a smile. "It's nothing at all."

"I'm afraid we need to do this," Sebastian added, looking at him blankly. Oliver had an old familiar feeling as he gazed at his dad and had no idea what he was thinking.

But what was he going to do, resist? Fight his way past these four adult vampires? His head fell. "Whatever," he muttered.

"All right, then," said Dr. Vincent, "I'll need you to roll up your sleeve."

As Oliver did so, Dr. Vincent flicked open the gold latches on his briefcase. Inside was a long syringe and a narrow glass vial. Dr. Vincent carefully picked up the vial. It held a ten-inch-long, squirming creature, with a maroon segmented body and over forty yellow legs. As it squirmed, it threw off bands of iridescent, rainbow-colored light.

"What's that?" asked Sebastian.

"Incan tomb centipede. It's a borderland creature that reproduces in multiple worlds at once. It's about to lay its eggs, which is why it's emitting force spectra like you see."

"That's interesting," said Phlox, but Oliver thought

he saw a shadow of discomfort pass across her face. Maybe she actually felt a little bit bad about seeing her son treated like a lab rat. *Not bad enough to stop it, though,* Oliver thought darkly.

Dr. Vincent took the syringe and pressed the long needle through the rubber stopper at the top of the vial. He speared the centipede, causing it to flail wildly. For a moment, Oliver felt some relief. At least the whole creature wasn't being put inside him. But a large needle full of its glowing innards was. The syringe filled with a swirling rainbow of juices.

"It's an amazing feat this little guy performs," Dr. Vincent was saying. "It suspends itself in a multi-world state, existing in up to fifty worlds simultaneously. It's the power to suspend that we are transferring to you. It will help you to acclimate to the Anointment."

Dr. Vincent traded the vial for a small kitchen blowtorch. Depressing the trigger created a small blue flame. "This will sting a bit," he said matter-of-factly, and proceeded to put the flame to Oliver's arm.

"Tssss!" Oliver flinched, almost falling off the chair, but Sebastian held him in place. A sour odor of searing flesh filled the room, and a small circle of Oliver's arm was burned to black.

"There we are," said Dr. Vincent, and immediately plunged the syringe into the burned spot. Luckily, Oliver could no longer feel any pain there, though the pain he'd already felt had left him shaking. He looked at Sebastian's stern face above, Phlox's concerned expression, even Tyrus's tense gaze, and hated them all. Watching him suffer, doing nothing.

Dr. Vincent depressed the syringe. Oliver felt a brief surge, and his vision blurred for a moment, then cleared.

"And that's it," said Dr. Vincent. "See? Nothing to it."

"What exactly did that do for him?" Sebastian asked quietly.

"Well," Dr. Vincent explained as he packed up his gear, "when Vyette Anoints Oliver, she is giving him transdimensional energy. When Illisius does come calling, Oliver will need to be able to travel through multiple worlds. No vampire has ever even fully left *this* world before. Once Oliver is out, he'll encounter different time states, forces he's never felt, and we don't want him to be torn apart in the process. Creatures like this centipede have adapted ways to hold their essence together despite the pull of different force parallels." He slapped Oliver on the back. "It'll keep him whole!"

Oliver wanted to scream. *This* was not what he needed to make him whole, not by a long shot.

✹

Oliver woke and left the house as quickly as he could Wednesday evening, but only reached the Aurora Bridge before he stopped. He didn't want to go to school, or anywhere else. His arm was still killing him, and a dull ache had spread up through his shoulder to his chest.

Beside him was the giant stone troll sculpture. Oliver climbed up the dirt embankment into the shadows behind its giant head, listening to see if there were any vampires already in this spot. Bane and his friends Randall and Ty used to hang out here all the time. *Run along, Lamb!* Bane would have shouted at him. Now the spot was silent, empty.

Oliver fished Bane's objects from his pocket. He opened the amethyst box and looked at the frozen firefly. "Speak," he said softly. "Hello? Can you tell me how to be free of all this?" The firefly didn't move.

Oliver closed the box and now examined the other object, the tiny parchment scroll. As he unrolled it, he frowned. It was six inches long and seemed to be full of writing, but most all of it was burned to black and unreadable. It had likely been an enchantment: the kind that could be used only once. Whatever it was, Bane had already done it. Except there was one last line at the bottom of the page that remained unburned. It was written in Skrit, but Oliver wasn't sure of the meaning. He pronounced each symbol aloud, slowly:

"*Revelethh . . . lucenthh . . . persechhh . . .*"

There was a flash of white light. Oliver squinted, his vision overwhelmed. He heard a faint hiss, like electricity, with soft sparks.

Hey. The apparition was sitting beside him on the dark slope. It was a figure about his height, made of white light edged in silver, and throwing off pale blue sparks. There were impressions of details, like jeans, a sweatshirt, and shaggy hair. It seemed to be a boy, but the face was impossible to see in the blinding bright.

Oliver wanted to shout, *Where have you been?* but he didn't, because, as had happened before, the apparition made him feel calm. *Hey,* he thought back at it, then asked his question politely, *Where have you been?*

I have to be summoned, the apparition replied.

Oliver looked down at the scroll. *I just did that, didn't I?*

Yes.

So, Bane was summoning you? Oliver sifted through his memories and realized that every time he'd seen the apparition, it had been around Bane.

Your brother was the one who brought me here to begin with.

Oliver looked down at the burned writing. *You're part of Bane's treachery.*

Yeah, and I can help you with this. The apparition reached down and touched the amethyst box. *Let me see it.*

Oliver flipped it open.

Watch. The apparition pinched its own forearm with

two fingers and pulled a small sphere of swirling white energy free as it had done to give Oliver tears. Oliver thought he felt a sensation of pain from it, as if doing this hurt. It reached over and placed the sphere onto the firefly. The light dissolved into the insect, and suddenly it began to glow pale green, and its wings buzzed to life. The firefly lifted off the felt, hovering in front of Oliver's face.

There was a sound of inhaling, like someone struggling to breathe. *Hello, Oliver*, a female voice said distantly, as if speaking on a distant radio station. But Oliver still knew the voice. Selene.

Say hi back, the apparition urged.

"Hi," Oliver said to the firefly.

Oliver, it whispered faintly, *in order to undo the prophecy, you must be made whole with what was lost yet lingers. This can be done in the company of what was taken, but only before the Anointment has been completed.*

The firefly went dark. With a slight hiss, its wings shriveled, its body curling into a tight ball, and it fell into the box, dead.

Oliver frowned. "What's that supposed to mean?" He looked at the silent insect. "I need more than that," he said, then turned to the apparition. "Do you know what that means?"

The apparition seemed to sigh. *I have an idea, but I have to go now.*

"Why?"

It's not safe.

"Not safe?" Oliver repeated. "What's not —" but then he noticed a hissing wind, growing louder. He recognized the sound and looked up.

Plumes of smoke were rushing down from the bridge, spiraling toward the street, and re-forming as vampires. Boots, long black coats, lapel pins made of bone . . . Half-Light.

"I have a reading! Behind the troll." It was Leah, her palms swirling in the air.

There were five of them, the kind of team that Sebastian used to lead. And there was one other among them: the tall, black-robed Reader with its single white eye.

Oliver. The apparition sounded dead serious. *They can't find out that you know about me. . . .*

"Set up the binding net!" Oliver heard Tyrus barking from below. He looked down to see Yasmin and the others flanking the troll.

Oliver scrambled to his feet. They'd be surrounded in moments. He backed up farther into the shadows beneath the bridge, spectralizing. *There's nowhere to go*, Oliver thought to the apparition.

Suddenly, another voice spoke in his head. *Don't worry, I've got you.*

Invisible hands yanked him backward, right out of the world.

✴

Oliver watched through veils of gray, like the world was beyond a dusty window, as the Half-Light vampires scoured the area where he had just been.

Sorry I didn't get there sooner.

Oliver turned, looking over the small hand on his shoulder. Jenette stood beside him, the gray beach of the Shoals stretching away behind her. *Thanks*, said Oliver.

Unlike in the physical world, where Jenette appeared as a misty presence wrapped in veils, here she had a small, delicate face and long chestnut hair that reached almost to her waist. She wore white flannel pajamas with tiny smiling frogs on them. She looked younger than Oliver by a year or two, and maybe a little too old to be wearing frog pajamas, but what Oliver was seeing now was Jenette's wraith-self, a mix of who she was at the moment she'd died, and a reflection of the passage of time since. How long had Jenette been dead and roaming as a wraith? Oliver guessed that it hadn't been that long, as ancient wraiths tended to look quite hideous, and Jenette was still —

Cute?

What?!

Jenette's eyes fell. *Ah, sorry, I just hoped you were going to say "cute."*

Um . . . Oliver tried to think of any kind of response.

Jenette glanced up sheepishly, blowing her bangs out of her eyes. *It's okay. No worries.*

Where's the apparition? Oliver asked.

The what?

You know, the — he tried to think of how to describe it — *the glowy thing. . . .*

Oh, him, ha. Jenette laughed. *Right. He's here. He lives in the Shoals, after all.*

He does? Oliver frowned at her. *You know what it is, don't you?*

Well . . . kinda. Jenette smiled. *I'm surprised you don't, actually, but you vampires are funny. You pride yourselves on a larger understanding of the universe, but then sometimes it's amazing what you don't get.*

Something fairly obvious finally occurred to Oliver: The apparition had been wherever Bane had been, but Jenette had been wherever the apparition had been as well. She was also the one who knew to find Bane in the forgotten graveyard, and the apparition had been there, too.

It's true, said Jenette, hearing his thought. *I've known him for a long time.*

So, Oliver thought, *Selene told Bane to summon the*

apparition, and it has something to do with undoing the prophecy. That's why Half-Light is after him. . . .

Yes, yes, and yes, Jenette replied.

But you're not going to tell me what he is.

He asked me not to, said Jenette. *But don't worry. You'll know soon enough.*

Great, Oliver muttered.

Oliver, don't be mad! Jenette glanced past him, back into the world, where Half-Light was still searching. *Come here,* she said, turning away.

What do you mean? Oliver asked, watching Jenette walk away down the beach.

I mean come with me, just for a minute. Please? I don't bite.

But — Oliver remembered the last time Jenette had brought him to the Shoals, a borderland between worlds. It had been just after Oliver had been struck by the Scourge of Selket, up in the Space Needle, and she'd had to struggle mightily to hold him here. Pulling a physical body out of the world was like pushing against an elastic band as far as it would go.

It's okay! said Jenette, walking up the beach. *Everyone is helping this time.*

Everyone? Oliver's eyes slowly adjusted to the hazy world around him. There was only endless gray sand and sky, and a brushstroke of brown grass along the dune's high peak . . . yet now Oliver began to notice other figures on the beach. Here and there, always alone, grown-ups and children of all ages, some sitting, staring out at the starry sea, others trudging along the water's edge. All were silent. All were barefoot. Each was clothed for a different season, wearing everything from shorts to parkas.

Oliver sensed that they were wraiths, spending forever here, resting between their grief-stricken visits into the world, or being held here by a Merchynt. If his gaze lingered for too long on one of them, it seemed to create a little ball of sadness in his gut, and so he tried to simply look straight ahead as he followed Jenette. Out of the corner of his eye, he noticed the wraiths turning their heads to follow his progress down the beach.

They walked along the hard sand at the water's edge. The world was bright, but there was no sun, only a sameness that made Oliver squint. The water lapping calmly onto the beach was black, dotted with stars, almost as if it was made of space itself.

Ahead, a jetty made of large chunks of rock had appeared from the fog. Jenette reached it and began hopping out over the stones. *Come on, Oliver!* she called almost playfully.

Oliver looked back, but the view of the troll was gone. There was only beach. He started after Jenette, leaping from one barnacle-crusted stone to the next. They were tilted at steep angles, slippery with cold, black algae.

Unseen water sloshed in the deep crevices. Oliver slipped and had to grab the edge of a rock to avoid falling in.

Waves bucked and dunked against the jagged rocks at the jetty's end. Jenette sat on a long, flat rock that stuck out over the sea like a tongue, her feet dangling. Oliver sat beside her.

How was Emalie's party? Jenette asked.

Oh, it was fine. You weren't there. Dean was supposed to invite everyone. . . .

He did. But I didn't come. I know I'm not Emalie's favorite, and it was her big night. . . . Jenette turned away and said quietly: *She would have wanted you all for herself.*

Oliver had no idea how to respond. He watched the starry depths below.

Not much of a view, huh? Jenette said moments later.

It's kind of amazing. You can feel the other worlds. . . . Almost like you could dive in and swim to them.

But you can't, Jenette muttered. *Not as long as you're a wraith. A vampire, either. You go out and swim in that water, and you could go and go and go, but sooner or later, you'll end up back on this beach. You can't leave this world, no matter how hard you try.*

That may change soon, Oliver said darkly.

Or not. Jenette gave him a motherly pat on the shoulder. *We don't want it to.*

Oliver looked back at the faint, lost-feeling wraiths.

The wraiths have a stake in your destiny, too, Oliver, Jenette explained.

Why? Wouldn't opening the Gate end your suffering? Oliver asked.

Ha, no. If the world were destroyed, we would be freed, but the loved ones, to whom our grief is attached, would be killed. We want to be at peace, but not at their expense.

Who is your grief attached to? I mean, is it okay to ask that?

Sure, said Jenette with a sigh. *It's my mom. I died in a house fire. It was just me and her. She survived, but trying to save me she got burned bad.* Jenette's heels stopped kicking. Her voice quieted. *Now she's in so much pain every day, and she feels so guilty that she couldn't save me. I used to visit her, try to tell her she did the best she could. I think she heard me, but then she started telling everyone around her that my ghost was haunting her. I only made things worse. So I stopped visiting. But then I couldn't leave the world. You know what they say; you don't know you're becoming a wraith until you are one. And now I'm owned by Spira,* Jenette finished glumly. *Being a wraith sucks.*

Listening to Jenette's story, Oliver had a strange flash of doubt about his human parents. What if he found them, only to frighten them? He'd always just assumed it would be a happy reunion, but how were they going to react to their son, gone sixty-four years, suddenly returning? Or what if it was great, but then Oliver wasn't able to undo the prophecy? Then knowing them would only make it worse. Oliver tried to put these worries out of his mind. *Sorry*, he said to Jenette.

Oh, it's okay, she replied. *Since I failed to slay you for the Brotherhood, Spira hasn't hired me out to anyone. Like I care. . . . It just means I can slip away and hang with you guys.* Oliver felt her look at him. *I really like being with you.*

Oliver gulped. *That's cool*, he said awkwardly.

Suddenly, there was a flash of black around him. For just a moment, he saw the troll, the rafters of the bridge.

We're running out of strength to keep you here, said Jenette. *But Half-Light's gone.*

Okay. Oliver stood. *Well, thanks for helping me.*

You're going to Emalie's after school, to do the Portal? Jenette asked.

Yeah. You, um . . . you can come, too, if you want.

Nah, said Jenette. *I'm going to stay here, with him.* She turned back to the beach. The apparition was in the distance, standing at the shoreline, skipping rocks.

Why don't I get to know what he is? Oliver asked again.

He's nervous about it, said Jenette. *He wants to wait until you're ready to understand.*

And when is that going to be?

Jenette smiled. *I think after the Portal you'll know.*

The Portal? What's that got to do with anything?

It has everything to do with everything, said Jenette. *Trust me. Trust us.*

The world flashed to black again, and Oliver found himself beneath the bridge alone. He headed for school, his arm still aching. All night, his thoughts kept leaping ahead to the Portal, making each hour of school pass even more slowly.

CHAPTER 6

Underneath the Christmas Tree

Oliver rushed into Emalie's basement after school to find her and Dean sitting on the floor. The lights were off. Pillar candles flickered in the corners and atop the washing machine. Emalie had a new set of photos hanging across the ceiling, shots she'd taken of a decrepit, vandalized motel that had recently been torn down.

"Hey," said Emalie, arranging objects in a circle of gypsum sand. "Things are just about ready." She looked up and paused. "What's that face for?"

"What face?" Oliver asked, sitting between them.

Emalie studied him. "It's, like, no-face. You're totally blank. Usually means something's bugging you." She smiled. "But it's sorta how you look all the time."

Oliver's small smile appeared for a moment, but quickly faded. "Check this out." He pushed up his sleeve and showed Emalie and Dean the black burn from the centipede injection. "There's more," he said, pulling out Bane's objects. He explained about the apparition and

Half-Light's arrival, and what Jenette said about the Portal.

"What does the Portal have to do with the apparition?" Emalie asked.

"I don't know," said Oliver anxiously. "Let's just do it." He glanced at Dean. "How's the hindrian charm holding up?"

"Pretty good, far as I can tell," Dean replied.

"I've been thinking about that," said Emalie, rummaging through her bag beside her, "and about how Half-Light said they'd be watching you." She produced a small green leaf. "There's something I want to try, before we do the Portal," she said. "I have an idea of where we can go and be sure nobody's listening."

"Cool, where?" Oliver asked.

Emalie looked up, and Oliver saw that her eyes were burning red, her pupils shining white. The leaf burst into flame, creating a tiny plume of fire that swirled up from her palm.

"Emalie . . ." Oliver began.

The column of flame flattened at its peak and branched out in three points, one aimed at each of them. . . . *"Bind!"* Emalie said, her voice edged with demonic hiss.

The fire burst in three directions at once. It struck Oliver, Dean, and Emalie in the chest, throwing them each back to the floor.

Oliver saw gray, and heard a distant roar, like falling water. He glanced around and for a moment panicked. There was a foggy sky, with treetops below him. But his feet were planted on a platform made of thick wooden boards. The giant arms of a great tree rose around them, branching into a wide canopy of leaves above. In the center of the platform, a small fire crackled.

Beyond the branches was a fog-shrouded world. This tree was far taller than any of the others. The rest of the forest seemed distant below them. Birds called, and Oliver smelled a pungent aroma of living and decaying. Something rushed as well, a river in the shadows far below.

"Where are we?" asked Dean, looking around.

"It's called the Delta," Emalie said. "It's another borderland, an edge of the world like the Shoals or the Yomi. That river below is Acheron, the one we crossed in the Underworld near Morosia."

"The one that Hades' Well fell into," said Oliver. He gazed below and spied the slight blur of a river squiggling among the thick jungle. Low clouds passed beneath, momentarily erasing his view. Oliver remembered his studies. "Oh, yeah, spirits that leave the world by Acheron pass through here, and the strongest make it to the sea beyond, where you leave the world."

"What happens to the others?" Dean asked.

As if in answer, something large and hungry growled in the forest shadows far below.

Oliver considered their high platform again. "What is this?" he asked Emalie.

"It's a place for council. It's connected to the deepest parts of our minds, to our sense of truth and trust, and it's totally private. Pretty cool, huh?"

"So this is, like, our private forest?" asked Dean.

"No," said Emalie, "the tree house is ours, but the forest is shared."

There was a fluttering of air, and they looked up to see some dark, winged figure soaring over their treetop. It arced down through the fog, then back up, and landed in the distance. Now Oliver could make out another tree out there, as tall as this one. A tiny fire crackled to life on a similar platform. And he saw others now, far in the distance, with little fires burning.

"You can rent them," Emalie said in explanation.

Oliver turned to her. "Rent? From whom?"

"I got this one from Sylvix. He's that Merchynt that I buy supplies from in the Yomi," Emalie said casually, as if a human going to the Yomi and dealing with a Merchynt was no big deal. It had been one thing when she'd had Jenette protecting her, but Oliver knew that now she just went on her own, and somehow had no trouble.

"How did you pay for this?" Oliver asked warily.

"Don't worry," said Emalie, avoiding his eyes.

"Emalie . . ."

"Just trust me, Oliver." She shot him a sharp glance.

"So," said Dean, "we're here in our minds, but, like, physically, we're still in the basement, yes?"

"Right," Emalie answered. "Our bodies are still there."

"Isn't that dangerous?" Dean asked. "When we traveled into Bane's head, our bodies got attacked by zombies while we were gone."

"We just have to be more careful," said Emalie.

"Okay . . ." Dean looked around and grinned. "This is cool, like a mental hideout."

"Yup," Emalie agreed. "Oh, and this is neat, too. Watch: Dean, have you been under Lythia's command since the night at the lighthouse?"

Dean shook his head. "No," he said.

And Oliver found that he believed him fully and completely. There was no doubt. "Wow."

Emalie smiled. "We can't tell lies here. This place is deeper than any lie can penetrate."

"How long do we have this place for?" Dean asked.

"You have to rent it a millennium at a time," said Emalie matter-of-factly, with a sly smile, "so I think we're good for a while."

"How do we get back and forth?" asked Oliver.

"Check your left wrist." She held out hers. On the tender skin below her palm was a small black mark, like a little tattoo, of a single, oval leaf. Oliver and Dean found that they had them, too. "You put two fingers on it and imagine this place. To get back, you reach out for your senses. You'll find them and return. But we need to do the Portal first."

"We can do that while we're here?" asked Dean.

"Yeah," Emalie explained. "You can bring supplies and do certain enchantments here," Emalie said, picking up her bag from beside her. "It's included in the rent. And we don't need our bodies for the Portal."

The three sat cross-legged around the fire. Emalie placed a small flat square in front of her: the negative of the photo she had taken of Oliver almost a year ago, which showed him as only a blur on the ceiling.

Next, she produced a slim black bottle. Désirée had given them this chemical, saying that it would help develop the photo. What it had really done was reacted with a portal that she had hidden within the Amulet of Ephyra. Emalie dabbed a drop of the shimmering silver liquid onto the blurry form of Oliver. There was a slight hiss and the liquid turned to steam, leaving the negative looking the same.

"And now for the Portal." What Emalie placed in the circle next caused a small ache in Oliver. It was the browned newspaper clipping from the night of Oliver's siring and his human parents' alleged death, with the title: CHRISTMAS TRAGEDY. Bane had kept this, along with other clippings and trinkets, at the grave of his own human parents.

"You sure it's ready?" Oliver asked.

Emalie nodded seriously. "I'm pretty sure the clipping is now a portal to the night you died."

"Pretty sure?" asked Dean.

"It was the best object to use, 'cause it was created so close to the actual date," Emalie explained. "Its natural properties didn't need much changing. And yeah, I mean, my aunt and I followed the steps. Now we just need to activate it." Emalie removed a small, yellow object from her pocket. It was thin, curved, and Oliver realized it was a fingernail.

"It was a little awkward getting this from Chronius," said Emalie, "but it should work. I just have to melt it. . . ." She placed the fingernail in a small metal camping mug and held it over the fire. "We'll definitely end up somewhere."

Oliver was still amazed to hear Emalie speak so casually about her growing powers. As if Sylvix wasn't enough . . . Chronius was a big time demon, who existed across fourth-dimensional space. He had to grant access on behalf of his demon race in order for anyone to use a time portal. That Emalie had gotten his permission, in the form of this fingernail, was impressive, and worried Oliver a bit, too. How did she do such things?

"Okay," said Emalie. She pulled the cup from the fire and poured the drops of melted fingernail over the negative.

Oliver felt a fresh rush of nervousness. After so much, they were finally going back again, to learn for sure this time. *My real parents . . .* He tried to contain his excitement.

Emalie closed her eyes and took a deep breath, then whispered in Skrit: "*Traversethh.*" It meant "to cross over." When her eyes opened, her irises had turned red again, her pupils glowing white.

A wind began to swirl in the tree. Silver light rose from the negative, stretching into a tiny rainbow until it reached the clipping. The light grew into an orb, the wind increasing until the rush of light and air enveloped them all. Details of the tree house washed away, fading within a formless white.

✿

There was a flash, and then Oliver found himself looking up at a nighttime scene. It took only a moment to recognize the downtown Seattle plaza, the old stone buildings and cobblestone streets of 1946, the large Christmas tree, the cold rain stinging his face. And leaning over him, the faces of Lindsey and Howard. *Mom . . . Dad . . .*

Something distracted them, then the world spun, blurring, and Oliver found himself floating above. Emalie and Dean were beside him, looking down at a huddled couple, fawning over the child, Nathan. Phlox crouched, Sebastian beside her, hand on her shoulder. And Nathan was screaming.

Phlox cooed quietly, then sank her fangs into his neck. The screaming ceased. Phlox pulled away. Nathan's face was peaceful and still, eyes wide like they were looking at something far away. Two red holes glistened in tender white skin.

As they had seen on their last journey, for a moment a faint white veil of mist rose and swirled above the child's face, then slipped away on the breeze.

Your spirit, Emalie uttered faintly.

What? Oliver turned to her.

That was your human spirit leaving, she said. *I could feel it.*

Oliver gazed back down at the scene, but the misty white was already gone. The thought filled him with sadness, imagining his spirit wandering alone, eventually drifting out of the world, or being devoured on its way, like in the Delta.

Phlox stood, wrapped the unmoving baby in a yellow blanket, and handed him to Sebastian, who tucked him carefully into his long coat. They shared an embrace, looking down at the tiny child with tender smiles, and then stole off into the night.

Oliver turned his gaze toward the Christmas tree. There, beneath its wide branches, were Howard and Lindsey, lying still on the pavement.

They're not dead yet, Dean reported, *but they're about to be.* He pointed. Two more vampires were emerging from a nearby manhole. They approached the tree. Oliver recognized Tyrus and Yasmin, looking younger.

They're here to finish the job, Oliver guessed. He felt the urge to stop them, but knew there was nothing to be done. They were merely observers in time.

Tyrus and Yasmin knelt by Oliver's human parents. Each pulled aside a shirt collar and bent over, fangs bared —

"Just a moment."

Another figure had appeared, standing beside the Christmas tree. A tall woman in a long lavender coat, wearing a wide-brimmed hat with a pink flower in it. At first, Oliver thought it was a vampire, but her scent was different. In fact, she didn't seem to have a scent at all.

"Whatever has happened here?" the woman asked innocently.

Is that . . . Emalie began.

Oliver recognized the voice, too, and understood that the innocent tone was a ruse.

"Désirée?" said Tyrus.

Oliver's insides burned with rage. Again he felt the helpless urge to intervene.

Tyrus continued, "We're just spreading a little holiday cheer."

Désirée smiled. "Tut-tut, Tyrus. You should know better than to lie to me. It's big business you're attending to this evening. The Underworld is aflutter with rumors about Half-Light tinkering with prophecies."

"Well," Tyrus said carefully, "it is what it is. Not my place to ask. We have our orders."

"Of course you do, which is why I didn't slay you immediately." Désirée's hand flashed from her pocket and bright red light burst forth, slamming into both Tyrus and Yasmin. They flew backward and crashed to the ground, out cold.

Désirée knelt between Oliver's human parents and put a hand to each of their throats. Warm light radiated from her palms, making brief, blinding discs. Then she stood.

"There we are," Désirée said to herself. She looked over her shoulder. "This way!" Three humans approached, dressed in leather bombardier jackets. "Thank you for coming," said Désirée. "I assume you have made the arrangements to reacquire these bodies before they are buried."

"We have," said one of them nervously.

"Excellent. Be prepared for them to be quite disoriented when they awaken."

The humans nodded.

"I'm sure it's obvious that you'll need to hide them very well, but not too well. They must be found, but not for a long time."

"Th-thank you," one of the humans replied.

"Of course. Your little group sounds like a fine cause. The Brotherhood of the Fallen, is it? Good luck with all that. Now — ah," Désirée's voice turned cold, "please don't do that."

One of the Brotherhood had produced a stake and was nearing Tyrus.

"I need them," Désirée explained. "When they wake up, I'll have fixed their memories so they'll go back to Half-Light and report that the parents were successfully dealt with. No one will be the wiser, as long as you fake the burial. Now, run along and alert the police."

The Brotherhood members hurried away.

Désirée watched them go, then strolled off down the street. The plaza was empty again, except for Oliver's fallen parents, appearing dead, and yet, not.

So, that happened, said Dean.

Yeah, said Oliver. It was something, but it didn't tell them where his parents were now, and it didn't tell them why Désirée would want them alive.

A police siren warbled in the distance.

So now what? Dean asked.

Oliver lowered toward the tree. He reached the ground, stepped past Tyrus and Yasmin, and slowly approached his parents' still bodies, stopping at their feet. They were so silent, eyes open to the rainy sky. His father, Howard, with a sharp chin, deep-set brown eyes. His mother, Lindsey, with a circular face and dark hair, her eyes hazel.

Emalie joined him. *You look like them*, she said. *Your dad's eyes, your mom's face.*

Oliver nodded. Even their scent seemed familiar, though he hadn't been with them in sixty-four years. He stared at their still faces, a faint white light playing on their cheeks —

Wait a minute. That light. Oliver turned toward the large Christmas tree.

There, cowering behind the trunk, hidden by branches and festive colored lights, was something small and white, a glowing sphere not much bigger than a goblet. Its edges sparked with electric blue. It hovered, quivering, as if it was alive.

Oliver . . . Emalie whispered.

It's my spirit, isn't it? Oliver asked. He felt a strange longing inside, as if he was looking at something he'd been missing. It shivered, almost like it was cold, or frightened. And yet, it made Oliver feel calm, too. The feeling was familiar.

It is, said Emalie.

Dean joined them, having to bend to peer beneath the branches. *Dude, that's your spirit? So why can we see it? I mean, when Emalie runs into spirits in the surface world, we can't see them.*

Because it's not leaving, maybe, Emalie offered. *Why isn't it leaving?*

Oliver gazed at the tiny glowing form. It edged around the tree, and then slowly floated forward, past Oliver, Emalie, and Dean, and lowered over Oliver's parents, lighting their still faces more brightly.

Pretty, isn't it? a woman's voice asked.

The light darted back into the branches, and the three looked up.

Désirée stood before them. She was still dressed in the styles of the 1940s, but how could she be speaking to them when they weren't even really there?

Désirée smiled at Oliver's thought, and there was something different about her face. It was still smooth and white, but her eyes had changed. Now they were glowing coins of gold, no pupils or irises, more like an insect. *You should know by now, Oliver*, she purred, *that what I do and how I do it is my business. Just like in my shop.*

Oliver felt a sudden burst of anger. *You slayed my brother!* he shouted.

Désirée shrugged her brow. *Oh, yes, that. But I also saved your parents. Complicated, I know. I have to admit, I am surprised to see you here. Quite impressive, Emalie.* She glanced into the tree, toward the spirit light. *And now I think you've seen just about enough.*

Désirée thrust her hand out and a wave of energy rippled from it.

Oliver, Emalie, and Dean were slammed backward and the past washed away. . . .

✦

Oliver wasn't sure where they'd end up, but Emalie's basement returned around them.

"Whoa," Dean gasped, "how did she do that?"

"No idea," said Oliver.

"Did you see her eyes?" Emalie asked, breathing hard. "What *is* she?"

"Something that even scares Half-Light," Oliver said, anger still coursing through him.

"So Désirée is working with the Brotherhood," said Dean, rubbing his head woozily.

"Or was, anyway," added Emalie. "They kept your parents alive and hid them. Why?"

"Don't know," said Oliver. Strangely, his thoughts weren't staying with his parents, or Désirée. "I wonder what happened to it. . . ." he thought aloud.

"To what?"

"My spirit," Oliver said quietly. Suddenly, he felt lost in his head, like he was walking around the base of a huge thought, but he couldn't quite make out what it was.

"A spirit is a soul, right?" Dean mused.

"Yeah," Oliver answered.

"But you're a vampire, so . . ."

"So," Oliver said, seeing more of the whole of this thought, "if I was like any other vampire kid, I would never have had a soul to begin with, 'cause I would have been made in a lab. But since I was sired, it would be different."

"What happens then?" Dean asked.

Oliver shuddered. "Well, when a vampire is sired, the human isn't totally dead —"

"Undead," added Emalie.

"Right. And the spirit stays around, like mine did in the Portal. It isn't free to leave until the demon arrives inside the human. When the demon takes control, that completes the vampire, and the spirit's last connection is broken. It would leave the world. Only . . ."

"That hasn't happened for you yet," Emalie finished.

"No," said Oliver. His chest felt tight. His fingers tingled. "I mean, so technically, since I haven't gotten my demon, my soul hasn't been totally freed from me yet. . . ." He trailed off.

"Then maybe your soul never left," said Dean. "Maybe it's still attached to you somehow."

"What was lost yet lingers," Oliver mumbled.

"Oliver . . ." Emalie said, her eyes widening.

Oliver dug into his pocket. He pulled out the felt bag, tearing at the drawstrings. He dumped the contents in his lap and unfurled the tiny scroll with shaking fingers.

"*Revelethh . . . lucenthh . . . persechhh . . .*"

There was a flash of light, and the apparition appeared beside them. Oliver turned to it, shaking, and yet there was that calm feeling, that same sense of familiarity.

Oliver, I told you it wasn't safe, the apparition said worriedly.

"It's okay," said Oliver quickly, desperate to hear his own words aloud. "I know what you are."

CHAPTER 7

Nathan's Window

"**D**ude, that's your *soul?*" asked Dean. "Right there?"

Oliver felt a sense of knowing, or relief, from the apparition. *Yes*, it replied. *You can call me Nathan. But Oliver, it's not safe. . . .*

"I know, you can't be here. *This* is Bane's treachery," Oliver explained to Emalie and Dean. "Bane summoned my soul. And Half-Light wants to destroy it."

"Back to the tree house?" said Emalie.

Oliver looked uncertainly at Nathan.

I can come there with you, he said.

Emalie pressed two fingers to the leaf on her wrist, then closed her eyes.

Dean and Oliver did the same, and returned to the platform above the jungle. The fire crackled in dusk light. Through the fog, the other fires glowed more brightly. Solitary bird calls echoed over the sound of the river below.

Oliver stared at the apparition, his soul. "You never left," he said quietly, "but, where have you been?"

"With our parents, at first," Nathan explained. Emalie and Dean could hear him now. "They couldn't see me, and most of the time they didn't know I was there. There were some quiet moments, when I think they could sense me in their presence. But it made them sad.

"So I'd leave now and then," Nathan continued, "and go to the Shoals. I was growing up at the same speed you were, but I never knew about you. I mean, I knew I was attached to someone. When you were lonely, or sad, I'd be sad, too, but I didn't get why. Then Jenette met you last winter. She and I were already friends, and at first, she thought you and I knew about each other, that we were even the same being . . . since, well, we are."

"That's what she meant," said Oliver, remembering when, in the Space Needle, Jenette had said: *You act like you haven't seen the Shoals before*. "She'd always say that she knew my feelings about my parents, but she meant *your* feelings."

"It was an easy mistake to make, since something like us has never really existed before. . . . Well, your brother had a lingering soul somewhere, but then he got a demon and it was freed. It probably never knew about him, just like I didn't know about you until Bane summoned me. Then I finally understood."

"Why didn't you tell me this the other night?" Oliver asked. "Or back on the bluff, or when Bane first summoned you?"

"Bane was going to explain it to you. Once he was gone, I — you're a vampire, you know. Vampires think souls are gross. I knew you were going to use the Portal, and I thought, if you saw me back then, leaving our body, and with our parents, you'd understand."

"My soul . . ." Oliver said again, not even sure what to make of it. All the years of feeling different, of having these emotions of worry, guilt, longing, and even hope. Had it all been because his soul had been out there, still attached to him?

"Yes," said Nathan. Oliver could feel him smiling, though he still couldn't make out Nathan's face.

"So . . ." Oliver almost didn't want to ask it. "There's a way for us to be rejoined?"

"Yes."

"And that will undo the prophecy?" Emalie asked.

"That's what Selene said," Nathan replied.

"The rest of her message," said Oliver. What was it? "Oh, right. *'In the company of what was taken . . .'* "

"What was taken from us," said Nathan.

"Our parents?" said Oliver. "You think?"

"I do," Nathan replied.

"And you . . . you said you stayed with them, so you know where they are?"

"I can show you right now," said Nathan, glowing brighter. "Come back to the basement, and we'll show you."

"Okay," said Oliver, dumbfounded. He nodded to Emalie and Dean. They touched their tattoos and focused. . . . The basement returned around them.

Jenette, said Nathan.

Jenette's smoky black form rushed into the room. *Hey, guys! This is so exciting!*

Two larger wraiths slithered into the room behind her and positioned themselves behind Emalie and Dean. *Ready?* Jenette asked from behind Oliver.

"Yeah. You guys?" he said to Emalie and Dean.

They nodded, and the wraiths pulled them back out of the world.

❋

Oliver found himself in the Shoals again, standing firmly on the endless gray beach with Emalie, Dean, Jenette, and Nathan. A crowd of wraiths stood around them.

It's this way, said Nathan, and he floated up the beach. They trudged through the sand after him. The wraiths parted to let them through, watching silently.

Ah . . . said Emalie, putting a hand to her temple.

What is it? Oliver asked.

Sadness, Emalie replied. *All around . . . I can hear them begging for help. It's hard to keep them out.*

Oliver reached over and rubbed her shoulder supportively.

It's up here, Nathan called. Oliver looked ahead to see Nathan climbing over the jetty. They followed. He turned and headed up the beach along the side of the jetty, toward the steep dune. At its base, bleached driftwood logs were scattered like giant bones. A small rectangular structure had been built from them. Nathan ducked through its cockeyed doorway.

Oliver had to bend far to fit into the structure, and Dean even more so. Emalie and Jenette crowded in behind them. There was nothing inside other than a flattened sand floor. Pale blue light fell on it, from a window that took up the entire back wall. But it wasn't a normal window. Oliver gazed into it and saw a world nothing like the Shoals.

There was a one-story house with a gently sloped, orange tiled roof and white walls. The lights were off, the nearby streetlights still on. A mailbox at the end of the driveway read 714. A cactus grew beside it. The road beyond curved to a cul-de-sac, surrounded by identical homes. In the distance, a jagged mountain range was silhouetted against a pale blue, predawn sky.

Is that . . .

Our parents' house, said Nathan.

Can we go? Oliver asked immediately.

You can't. Not from here.

Oliver nodded. He'd known the answer, but couldn't help asking. His body was still attached to the world back in Emalie's basement.

There's a street sign, said Emalie, pointing. *Saguaro Drive.*

The saguaro cactus grows in the Southwest, said Dean. *We just need Google maps and we're golden.*

If you can get there, said Nathan, *I can meet you there.*

And that will undo the prophecy? Oliver asked, scared to really believe it. He stared at the house. A car slowly drove by, flinging a newspaper that slapped onto the driveway. His house. His *home*. It was right there. Looking at it made his chest tight. He turned and ducked out of the driftwood house. He felt like he needed air. He heard shuffling as the others joined him.

You'll have to escape your vampire parents, said Nathan.

Not a problem, said Oliver, his thoughts racing. He would head to school like any other night. . . . *As long as I'm there for attendance first period, I can probably get away without anyone realizing. We can grab a Charion and be gone by dawn.* He felt a rush saying these things. Finally, making his own plan, for his own future.

It might be safer to take surface trains or buses, said Emalie.

You mean because once they figure out I'm gone they'll be looking for me, Oliver agreed. *Good point.*

That, said Emalie, *and the fact that we're coming with you.*

Emalie —

Don't bother, Oliver, said Dean. *We're going. The only question is, when?*

We have to leave before Friday, said Oliver. *Then they can't do the Anointment without me, and once we undo the prophecy, it will all be over.*

What about Désirée and Lythia?

We have to avoid them, too. The sooner we leave, the less chance we have of tipping anyone off to our plans. . . . How about tomorrow?

My aunt Kathleen can go with us, said Emalie. *Dean, will that be cool with your parents?*

I'll have to check, Dean replied. *Let's meet at my place.*

Is it really this easy? Oliver asked.

Emalie smiled. *Maybe not everything has to be hard.*

Oliver couldn't believe what they were saying. *Tomorrow night, then . . .* He stood there on the gray beach at the edge of the world, and looked from Emalie, to Dean, to Nathan, to Jenette. A great sense of energy filled him, a surge of purpose. This was his chance, his moment. To undo his destiny, to change his existence, to start over . . . whole. The faces staring back at him were bright in agreement.

We can do this, said Emalie. *Right?*

Sure, said Dean. *Tomorrow, we'll save the world.*

Okay. Oliver nodded. *It's a plan.*

CHAPTER 8

The Final Journey

Oliver spent most of Thursday sleepless, his mind churning over what was to come. And yet, finally, instead of lying there dreading the future, he could barely wait for it.

After they'd returned from the Shoals, they'd found his parents' street outside of Tucson, Arizona, and mapped the route. They would take buses to Los Angeles, then Phoenix. The hard part for Oliver would be hiding from the sun, but during daylight hours, he could sleep in the luggage compartments beneath the bus, or hang out on the ceiling. The hard part for Emalie and Dean would be convincing their parents to let them go. They were going to have to tell them about the prophecy. How would that go? Aunt Kathleen had promised to help.

Oliver imagined the bus ride, noxious with the scent of close-packed humans and exhaust. Sitting beside

Emalie, Dean across the aisle, playing cards, sharing earbuds . . .

Could he really escape the watchful eyes of his parents and Half-Light? He thought there was a good chance. They would be south of Portland, Oregon, by the time the school night ended, and closing in on California by the time Oliver was missed at dinner and the suspicions began. There were vampires in other cities, of course, and once Half-Light knew that Oliver was on the run, they would alert the entire New World.

But Half-Light would have no idea where he was going. They didn't know Oliver's parents were alive. By the time the daylight hours had passed on Friday, he would be heading toward Phoenix. Half-Light's hunt would be full-scale, but Jenette would be watching, and she and the wraiths could pull them into the Shoals to hide from any pursuing vampires. And the Darkling Ball would pass without him, without the Anointment, and meanwhile, Oliver would be nearing Tucson.

And what would happen when Oliver reached his parents' home? How would the prophecy be undone, and what did it mean to be joined with his soul? *I'll be more human, more like . . . her.* Oliver thought of Emalie. Her tears on her birthday. He'd be able to feel more of what she felt, of *how* she felt. And what would he be then? Surely not a vampire, because a vampire couldn't have a soul. Maybe something entirely new, something more whole, with real parents and a future before him that was unwritten.

Oliver couldn't believe the possibilities. There would be no more sleeplessness, no more worries, no more destiny he'd never asked for. He would get to start all over again. To be someone new.

Only a single evening of his old life remained. Compared to ending the world, it sounded like no problem.

✱

Oliver entered the kitchen for breakfast as usual on Thursday evening.

"How are you feeling?" Phlox asked. "Does your arm still hurt?"

"It's fine," Oliver replied. He sucked down his frozen mocha shake and ate his piece of serpent loaf as quickly as he could. "Gotta go," he said, sliding off his chair.

"Be home right after school," said Sebastian, emerging from the living room. "You'll need a good day's sleep for the Ball."

"Sure." Oliver turned to leave. He moved to the hall, slipped on his sweatshirt, slung his backpack over his shoulder — and, for just a moment, paused. This was it, after all. Good-bye. Oliver had no idea if he'd ever see them again, or what would happen to Phlox and Sebastian when he was discovered missing. *They can take care of themselves*, Oliver assured himself. That was true.

But they loved me. That was maybe also true, and yet, hadn't they chosen the prophecy instead of him, over and over, even after it had taken Bane? *But they'll miss me, won't they? Will they even be my parents anymore?* Oliver felt a moment of tightness. He hadn't expected these feelings.

"Something wrong?" Phlox sounded concerned.

Oliver only turned halfway around, so his face wouldn't betray his nerves. *You have to sound like nothing's changed*, he reminded himself. "Everything's fine," he said carefully, trying to imitate his sulk from earlier in the week.

"All right," said Phlox. "Have a good night."

"Yup." Oliver started down the stairs. *They were never even my real parents*, he assured himself. *And they never really understood me.* He hurried out the door, and as he left 16 Twilight Lane, he didn't look back.

✸

Oliver got to class early again. Attendance was taken at the start of the night. If Oliver wasn't in homeroom, Mr. VanWick would note it, and the office would call home. After that, though, none of the teachers would be reporting absences. There was any number of reasons why a kid might not be in class.

He sat quietly before class began, listening as his classmates discussed the latest developments in finding dates for the Darkling Ball. Seth had apparently been turned down by Carly, Suzyn had rejected Maggots in favor of going with Amelya, and Berthold was bringing his mom.

And he listened intently to Mr. VanWick's history lecture, as he normally would. Today they were covering a few of the classic Waning Sun traditions, such as the Gathering ritual performed by the vampires of the Arctic Underworld city of Issilya, beneath the polar ice, and the Thirty Days Thirty Bites ceremony that was regaining popularity in Bolivia.

Oliver went with his class to Music, and for the next half hour, he sat with his cello as they played a piece called "Sunset Finale." Drawing his bow slowly over the vibrating strings, Oliver momentarily forgot about the night's plans and just enjoyed the sounds. It was a pretty piece. So sad and complex. Would he still find it so once he had a soul? Or would he seek out happier, more human music? Would he still be good at the cello? *Of course I will,* he thought, frustrated by his own questioning. It wasn't like he was going to forget thirty-two years of cello training just because he had a soul. If anything, he'd probably feel the music more deeply.

Class was dismissed for Multi-World Math. Oliver loitered outside the music room door, until the rest of the kids were in their rooms. He turned to an old photo on the wall, of the human school chorus from long ago. He looked at the young teacher standing beside her class, her lovely face bright with a smile. When he'd found this photo almost a year ago, he hadn't known she was his human mother, Lindsey. *I'm on my way*, he thought nervously.

Oliver checked up and down the hall, then took off his heavy backpack and pushed it deep into a nearby trash can. He spectralized and slipped out the back door, into the night.

✦

Dean, Emalie, and Aunt Kathleen were waiting in the living room at Dean's house. Tammy, Mitch, and Cole were sitting together, talking quietly. The room hushed when Oliver entered.

"Hey, Oliver," said Dean.

"Hey." Oliver looked at the adult faces and saw their worried expressions. He could sense the complicated feelings in the room. The scents of fear and concern, the touch of anger.

We told them about the prophecy, Emalie thought to him.

How'd it go? Oliver thought back. He saw Mitch picking at his fingernails. Only Tammy had made eye contact with him so far.

"Everyone understands," Aunt Kathleen said quietly. "Obviously, no one is comfortable with this."

A small, frustrated sigh escaped from Cole. His eyes flashed over Oliver coldly. *Yes you are*, Cole had said when Oliver tried to say he wasn't dangerous. Indeed, he was.

"But," Aunt Kathleen added, "no one's comfortable with the world ending, either."

"I'm sorry," said Oliver, looking around the room.

No one replied.

After an endless moment, Tammy finally spoke. "So go, then. The sooner you leave, the better chance you'll have." She shot to her feet and hurried into the kitchen. "I made you some food to take."

"Thank you," said Emalie.

"Right," said Dean. "Okay, let's do it."

Cole stood and hugged Emalie tightly. "I wish I could help, somehow," he said, his chin resting atop her head. "Be safe."

"I will," Emalie replied.

Oliver wanted to say something more to them, but could tell that it was best to keep quiet. He was the reason for all of this danger and worry. He'd just make it worse if he opened his mouth.

"I'll do everything in my power to protect them," said Aunt Kathleen, wrapping a shawl around her shoulders.

"And I've alerted the Orani network. We'll have friends along the way."

"Here are your snacks," said Tammy, hurrying back. She wrapped Dean in a hug. "Be careful, honey."

"Okay, Mom," said Dean.

Oliver stood alone, watching the good-byes, and felt a fresh wave of guilt.

They left out Dean's back door, weaving through yards, keeping beneath trees to avoid the eyes of occupied animals, then caught a human taxi to the bus station.

✴

"**N**orthwest Trailways forty-three now departing for Yakima, Tri-Cities."

Oliver, Emalie, and Dean dropped their bags on a long bench by a newsstand. Tall windows behind them looked out at the silver grilles of arriving and departing buses.

"Who wants snacks?" asked Aunt Kathleen. "They probably don't have blood," she said with a forced smile, "but I saw candy and hot dogs and the like."

"A hot dog could work," said Dean, "that's practically zombie food anyway."

"Fries," said Emalie, then turned to Dean, "and *yuck*."

"I'll stay here with our stuff," said Oliver.

"You want anything?" Emalie asked.

"Belgian chocolate would be good."

"Oliver, it's a bus terminal."

"Coke, then." He pulled a tiny plastic jar from his bag. "I brought some cayenne for it."

Emalie wrinkled her nose at him. "Weirdo."

The three headed off.

"Northwest Trailways one-ninety-two now arriving from Vancouver."

Oliver sat sideways on the bench, watching the buses pull in and out, their brakes whining, their wipers removing a final spray of rain. One pulled up now and as the lights brightened inside, the marquee on top scrolled from Seattle to Portland to San Francisco.

That was their bus. Oliver felt a nervous rush. He glanced quickly around the station again, eyes alert for vampires, but there was nothing, same as it had been all night. Oliver checked the clock. It was nearing lunchtime at school. Half-Light might still have no idea that he was gone. *Are we really going to make it?* he wondered, and the thought filled him with fear, but the feeling was electric: Finally, he feared something unknown instead of something chosen for him. This bus ride was just the beginning of a whole new future.

He watched groggy people getting off the bus and making their way inside. They squinted at the bright lights, most heading toward the bathrooms. Some were met by loved ones. A dad with a daughter, meeting a wet-eyed woman. A girlfriend and boyfriend embracing passionately.

Outside, the driver was checking the cargo compartments for baggage left behind.

"Northwest Trailways eight-twenty-two to San Francisco will begin boarding in five minutes."

Oliver's head whipped around, scanning the station, his nose working intently. But there was still nothing. Not a trace of a vampire. There was a zombie woman, leaning against the wall by the bathrooms, but that wasn't surprising. Since zombies weren't allowed onto Charions unless traveling with their masters, they sometimes used human buses. Actually, many zombies preferred just to pack themselves into a sturdy box and have themselves shipped places, as the care and cleaning that it took to make themselves presentable for being in close contact with humans on a bus was usually much more trouble than it was worth.

"Here's your Coke," Emalie said as she and Dean returned. "Aunt Kathleen is grabbing a magazine." They sat beside him.

"Thanks." Oliver added the cayenne to the can. His fingers were shaking slightly.

"You all right?" Dean asked.

"Yeah," said Oliver, but his insides were tied in knots.

Emalie rubbed his shoulder. "We just need to get on the bus. One thing at a time."

"Right," Oliver agreed, but something else was bothering him. He looked warily around the station again. There was still only the single zombie by the bathroom. Otherwise, nothing. *We just need to get moving*, he thought to himself. *Then, I'll be fine.* He was just nervous about the unknown. To change his destiny, to find his parents, to start a new future, it was big stuff. Of course he was anxious about it.

But was that really what he was feeling? Oliver craned his neck, scanning the station again. He almost bumped a traveler who was sitting down beside him.

"Oliver, relax," said Emalie.

But he couldn't. "Something's not right," he said.

"What?" Dean asked.

"I don't know," Oliver muttered. "It's just —"

"Too easy?" said a voice from beside him.

Oliver spun, recognizing the voice instantly.

"Hello, Oliver," said Braiden Lang, sitting next to him, legs crossed casually. He wore a black sweatshirt and military green jacket over his short, round frame, and had curly brown hair.

"What are you doing here?" Oliver snapped.

"I'm here for the going away party," said Braiden with a cold smile. "I would have appreciated a thank-you card, by the way. I mean, I am the one who told you your parents were alive in the first place."

"After you tried to kill us," muttered Emalie.

"Well, sure, but that was a long time ago." Braiden smiled, then gazed around the terminal. "So, funny that no one else is here to see you off. That's what's bothering you, isn't it?"

"You —" Oliver began, but Braiden was right. That was exactly what was troubling him.

"Yes," Braiden continued, "Oliver's off to undo his prophecy and save the world, and Half-Light didn't even send flowers. I wonder why that is."

"Maybe because we fooled them," offered Dean.

"Hah," Braiden chuckled derisively. "Right. Except here I am. So if *we* knew what you were up to, and we're just a little old bunch of humans, how is it that Half-Light doesn't?"

"What are you saying?" Emalie asked angrily.

"What I'm saying is that your boyfriend here is the most important vampire in the universe right now. Centuries of study and research have been put into Oliver's development, the ultimate instrument to fulfill Half-Light's sole purpose of opening the Gate. Everything they've worked for rests on tomorrow night, on the Anointment, on you, Oliver. Am I right?"

Oliver had to agree. "Yeah."

"So then, with everything you know about Half-Light, the same Half-Light that planned to slay your brother for disobeying their wishes . . . Do you really think they'd have taken their eye off you for even a second? Do you really think they'd just let you run away right before the biggest night in their history?"

Oliver looked desperately to Emalie and Dean. Their brows were furrowed in thought, and their heads had fallen just enough to show that they were thinking the same thing he was. "No," he said.

"Northwest Trailways eight-twenty-two to San Francisco is now boarding."

"But," said Dean, "we're just about to get on the bus. So where are they?"

Braiden looked around. "My point exactly."

Oliver spoke quietly. "They're letting us go."

"Letting us?" Dean exclaimed. "Why?"

Braiden held out a small piece of paper.

"What's that?" Oliver asked warily.

"It's just an address. Trust me."

"Yeah, right," muttered Oliver, but he took it.

"Be there at two A.M," said Braiden. "You'll see everything you need to see."

"But —" Oliver glanced back toward the bus. The journey, his parents . . .

"Think, Oliver," said Braiden. "Why would they let you go?"

< 111 >

Oliver felt stuck in place. He knew the answer, but he didn't want to admit it. He just wanted to keep thinking about the bus ride and Saguaro Drive. . . .

"The only way they'd let him go was if they didn't need him," mused Dean.

"Because they could fulfill the prophecy without him," added Emalie dejectedly.

"But how?" Oliver managed to say.

"The address," said Braiden, standing up. "Afterward, you know how to contact us."

"Wait," said Oliver.

Braiden turned back. "Yes?"

"Why are you helping me?"

"Because we can't get into the Darkling Ball to stop what's about to happen," said Braiden. "Back when your brother was being Anointed, we had the element of surprise. Not this time. So, unlike Half-Light, *we* still need you, Oliver."

"That's funny," Oliver muttered.

"There's nothing funny about it," said Braiden. "Our mission is to keep the Gate closed. That's *your* goal now, too, Oliver. So we're no longer enemies." Braiden nodded to the paper in Oliver's hand. "Go see what I mean." He turned and left.

Oliver stared blankly down at the paper. He unfolded it: 7002 SEAVIEW AVE. DOCK 7.

"We can't really trust him, can we?" asked Dean.

"If Half-Light has a way to fulfill the prophecy without you —" Emalie began.

"Then nothing we're about to do matters," Oliver finished. "We weren't going to make it to my parents' house before the time of the Anointment. And if they have a way to do it without me, then we wouldn't be able to undo the prophecy anyway."

"But how can they do that?" asked Dean. "*You're* Half-Light's last chance, right?"

Oliver couldn't respond. He felt the urge to run again, to get on the bus anyway. Emalie squeezed his arm. "You know we have to check it out."

Oliver nodded solemnly. That old feeling had returned: the feeling of having no choice, no say in anything.

"Final call for Northwest Trailways eight-twenty-two to San Francisco."

Aunt Kathleen returned. "Ready to go?" she asked, then noticed their ashen faces.

As Emalie explained things to her, Oliver stared out the tall windows, watching the bus driver slap the cargo doors closed and follow the last passenger on. The engine rumbled to life, and the doors squealed closed. There was a loud hiss, and the bus backed away in a slow, wide arc. Faces stared out the rain-streaked windows. Oliver imagined himself there, beginning the journey toward his freedom, his future. . . .

The bus rolled away into the dark.

CHAPTER 9

The Backup Plan

Oliver, Emalie, and Dean sat on the roof of a city bus, crossing Ballard. Aunt Kathleen had returned to Dean's house to update their parents.

This doesn't change everything, Emalie thought to Oliver. *I mean, we're delayed, but we can still find your parents, after.*

If there is an after, Oliver thought glumly, staring out at the cold, wet, choiceless world.

"We're coming up on the address," Dean reported. To their left, hundreds of sailboats and yachts bobbed in the dark. The breeze was sticky with salt, and tasted sour.

The three leaped off, over a high fence and into a nearly empty parking lot. To their right, a security booth stood beneath a streetlight. Staying in the shadows, they approached the docks. Water lapped and sloshed against the boat hulls. In the distance, a strange yelping sound pierced the night, like the barking of many dogs.

"Sea lions," said Dean. "There's a colony that lives out on the breakwater."

"You and all your animal trivia," Emalie teased.

"Well," said Dean, "it's actually zombie trivia. Sea lion brains are —"

"Okay, eww," said Emalie. "No more, please." Her watch made a tinny beeping sound. "Two A.M.," she announced.

A car engine reached their ears. They turned to see a long limousine entering the lot.

"That's probably who we're here to see," said Oliver.

"What's with vampires being so punctual?" Dean asked.

"We like neat numbers," Oliver replied.

The limo stopped at the far end of the lot. Doors opened and shut. Two vampires started out onto one of the docks. Two more remained by the car, standing guard.

"This way," said Oliver. He led the way out onto the nearest dock, number thirteen, then hopped up onto the bow of a small yacht. They slipped along its side, then jumped over a canal to a boat on the next dock. They crossed this dock to the next boat, and jumped again.

They reached dock seven and crouched on the stern of a sailboat. At the dock's end was a giant yacht, long, sleek, its window tinted black. The two vampires stood below it.

"Hello, Gentlemen." Malcolm LeRoux appeared on the yacht deck. The two vampires levitated up and followed him inside.

"Come on," said Oliver, but Emalie grabbed his arm.

"They'll have security."

"Then what do we do?" asked Dean.

"I'll go," said Emalie. "I can be invisible to vampires. You guys can watch from the tree house." She pulled back her sleeve to reveal her tattoo. "Meet me there."

They sank back, and reappeared around the fire. It was night in the Delta now, the fires on other platforms bright in the fog. The forest world was hidden below, the river gurgling unseen.

"I think from here I can use the conduit charm to bring you guys along with me, in my head." Emalie pulled off her necklace and held the tiny red beetle scarab in her palm. Then she held out her hands for Oliver and Dean to join in a circle. She blew on the hand with the charm, then closed her eyes.

There was a sense of movement. Oliver saw the docks again, but now through Emalie's eyes. He felt her mind tighten a bit as she concentrated, and then the world flickered just slightly as she made herself invisible.

Emalie jumped down to the dock, neared the yacht, and levitated to the deck. Ahead was a set of doors into the warmly lit cabin. Above was a second deck, and then a small top deck with a captain's wheel. A vampire stood there. It was Leah.

This will be a cinch, Emalie thought.

Oliver noted that confidence in Emalie's voice that she got during moments like this. She almost sounded excited about the danger. Like it fed her.

Come on, she said, hearing his thoughts. *This stuff is cool.*

Maybe to you, Oliver thought back. All he felt was worry.

Emalie entered the boat, passing through an elegant living room. Other than a slight side-to-side rocking motion, they could have been in an apartment building somewhere. There was a dark wood bar with a pewter carafe and goblets. A large, medieval oil painting hung on the back wall.

Ahead was a spiral staircase. *Down*, Oliver guessed. Emalie agreed, and descended to the deck below, entering a narrow hallway. Candles in glass vases were mounted on the dark, wood-paneled walls. The hall ended at a door, white light bleeding from its edges. Voices echoed from behind it. Emalie approached the door and with another tightening of concentration, she stepped through it.

The small room was bathed in white light. The walls were lined with steel tables and glass cabinets crowded with bottles, tinctures, and machines. A steady beeping sounded. Malcolm stood, arms folded. Beside him was Tyrus, holding a file folder.

"What do you think, Doctor?"

Dr. Vincent was bent over, a syringe in one hand, and in the other, Oliver recognized the vial with the writhing centipede. "I think it's taking," he said. "We can be fairly certain."

Sitting before the doctor, in a wheelchair, was a young vampire boy. Oliver guessed he was about fifty, fourteen vampire years younger than Oliver. He wore a white hospital gown, and stared up toward the ceiling, his eyes vacant. His arms and legs were strapped to the chair with thick leather restraints.

"How can we be certain of anything?" Malcolm scoffed. "It's impossible to know what's going on in there."

"Well . . ." Dr. Vincent turned to the counter and exchanged the syringe and vial for a small device the size of a cell phone. He held it close to the boy's face. Three spindly metal fingers extended from the device's top and sides. Their sharp tips moved directly toward small black holes on the boy's face, one on each cheek and one on the forehead. They sank into his white skin. The boy began to shake lightly, but his eyes remained open, empty. Tiny arcs of rainbow color began to swirl around his face.

"Force resonance readings are exactly where they should be," reported Dr. Vincent. "I see strengthening in all the areas necessary to receive the Anointment —"

"Nnnn." The boy began to vibrate, humming like a motor. His wrists and ankles strained the straps. His eyes remained blank.

"Nothing to worry about," said Dr. Vincent, but he looked concerned as he typed on the gadget. The metal fingers popped free and receded.

"What's happening to him?" asked Tyrus.

Malcolm only stared at the boy. His eyes had begun to glow faintly with a shade of crimson. "Alexy," he murmured.

Dr. Vincent now traded the gadget for a thick white glove and a small black jar. His jaw was set seriously. "More fragmentation of his mind, disrupting his nervous system," he said as he unscrewed the little jar. He reached in with two fingers and pulled out a slim, slippery brown creature. It writhed in his fingers, drops of tan liquid spraying the doctor's white coat and Alexy's trembling face.

"What is that thing?" Malcolm asked.

"Lake Naenia leech. We need to quell the tremors, stabilize the force patterns." Dr. Vincent carefully bent and held the squirming creature over Alexy's nose, then let it go. The leech disappeared into his nostril.

"DAH!" Alexy blurted. He jumped violently, the wheelchair momentarily leaving the ground. Then he slumped. The tremors had stopped.

"The boy is in no condition for this!" Malcolm protested. "He never has been!"

Dr. Vincent now held a long, narrow set of tweezers. He slipped them gingerly into Alexy's nostril, and then slowly pulled the leech free. It wriggled limply. "Well, this was never the ideal plan, Malcolm."

"All of your reports said that Nocturne would work," Malcolm sneered. "We never should have needed Alexy at all."

"What can I say, Gentlemen?" Dr. Vincent began to pack his briefcase. "The very foundation of science is trial and error, same as it is for the universe. We've done our best, and I think we will succeed. Now then." He grabbed his coat. "We'll see you tomorrow night."

"Apparently we will," Malcolm muttered.

Get out, said Oliver.

Right. Emalie retreated through the door and back to the dock. As she reached the sailboat deck, Dean and Oliver dropped hands at the tree house and returned to their bodies.

Footsteps clopped on the dock. They ducked as Tyrus and Dr. Vincent strode past. Then Oliver led them away, jumping from boat to boat. He stopped on another sailboat deck three docks over to wait until the limousine pulled away.

"They lied, to me, and my parents," Oliver said bitterly. "Of course they had a backup. Just like they had me, in case things didn't work out with Bane."

"Dude," said Dean, "that kid was seriously messed up —"

But Dean didn't finish. He was struck from behind by the boom of the sailboat they were sitting on.

"Don't talk about Alexy like that," a voice hissed.

Oliver and Emalie turned to see four figures landing on the sailboat cabin. Two zombie boys, a zombie girl, and —

"He's my brother," snarled Lythia LeRoux, "so be kind."

Oliver felt a surge of rage, but before he could react, the zombies had him. Lythia leaped down onto Dean, pulled him up by the head with a tearing of hair, and ripped the hindrian necklace from his neck, tossing it into the water.

"Rise, minion." Still gathering his wits, Dean stood, and when he looked at Oliver and Emalie, it was as if he didn't even know them.

"Tie them up," she ordered, "and then we'll talk."

CHAPTER 10

Uneasy Alliances

"**I** thought you were leaving town," Lythia muttered sourly. Her usual sly attitude was gone, and the way she paced back and forth across the deck of the sailboat suggested that she wasn't feeling like her usual playful self, either.

"What do you — *cough* — care?" Emalie wheezed, barely able to breathe against the thick, rusted chains that held her and Oliver to the mast of the boat.

Lythia sighed. "Blood bag," she said to Emalie, "I thought those chains would be tight enough that you'd have suffocated by now."

Don't try to talk, Oliver urged.

"What did I tell you, Nocturne?" Lythia continued. "Remember, way back in Harvey's? That I was here to save you — Lythia to the rescue, and all that. And there you were, off on your way to find your parents and be with your soul and yay rah rah! It was perfect. Half-Light has Alexy, anyway, so you would have been free as a bird. But, no, here you are again."

"You slayed my brother," Oliver growled, fighting the chains.

Oliver expected one of Lythia's typical sarcastic comebacks, but instead she lunged, landing beside Oliver, her face inches from his. "Yeah, I did. And you know what? You're the lucky one. How'd you like to have a brother like *that*?" She waved her hand back toward her father's yacht. "Maybe if you and your brother weren't such screwups, Half-Light wouldn't have had to make another prophecy vampire. Maybe *my* brother wouldn't be so messed up!" Lythia's eyes burned lavender.

Oliver tried to glare back at Lythia, but his anger was fading. Now he found himself asking, "What happened to him?"

Lythia stood up and looked away. "Everything started out fine," she said. "I remember the night my parents came home with little Alexy, freshly sired. They put him in a tiny wicker basket of soil. I sat by it all night, waiting for him to rise, and finally he started flailing and crying.

"We had twenty lovely and wicked years together," Lythia continued, "before that white knight of a doctor came along to start the force treatments. I could hear my dad grumbling, about how the *other one* — that would be you, Nocturne — was having issues, not sleeping and being all-around pathetic. So they started prepping Alexy to take your place, just in case. Only not everyone's made for that kind of thing. You may be a pathetic, sniveling drip, Nocturne, but your force signatures were strong enough to withstand the good doctor's treatments. But not Alexy . . ."

Lythia slammed her fist against the sailboat mast. "He was twice the cunning vampire that *you* ever were, but his forces got out of balance. Little by little, he didn't learn like the other kids, never got his words right, acted violent. He had to be restrained, locked up, until it all just broke down. Now look at him." She glared at Oliver. "And it's your fault."

"It's not!" Oliver protested. He couldn't believe what he was hearing, and how confused it made him feel. "It's Half-Light's fault."

"Yeah, well, true. It's theirs, too. Everyone's a bit to blame. That's how it always goes, isn't it?"

"Yes, master," the large zombie boy said dutifully.

"Oh, shut up!" Lythia whirled and shoved the zombie off the boat. He crashed into the water with a tremendous splash. "Anyway, so there you have it. Lythia has a screwed-up brother, too. Join the club." She paced away again.

Oliver watched her, wondering so many things. He'd thought all month about the moment when he'd see her again . . . but he'd never imagined it going like this.

Lythia stalked back toward them, the other zombies giving her a wide berth. "They think Alexy's already gone, that his mind is fried," Lythia said quietly, "but he's not. When I'm alone with him, and we talk — well, it's me doing all the talking, which is never a problem — I see him in there. He *hears* me. But he won't for much longer." Lythia shook her head sharply. "Not after tomorrow night. After they fill him up with bona fide Anointment powers, it's gonna blow his gaskets. Good-bye, brother. But all they care about is . . . well, you know all about that, don't you?"

Oliver nodded. As much as he couldn't believe it, he was looking at Lythia and his fury was turning into . . . understanding? So now what? What was he supposed to do with *that* feeling?

You're doing great, Emalie thought to him. *You've almost gotten her to admit what she's really up to.*

"Oh, I know that face," said Lythia, her eyes narrowing. "Blood bag over there is playing mind footsies with you, isn't she?" Lythia clasped her hands together. "It's love, isn't it? 'Cause *that's* gonna work out. A human girl and a vampire boy. Ha."

Oliver struggled to think through what Lythia was saying. It wasn't easy. Some of his anger was still floating around inside, and Lythia's demon presence always made his head feel foggy. He had to focus! The Anointment was going to ruin Alexy's mind. . . .

Half-Light didn't care. . . . Lythia thought he could *hear* her. . . .

There it is, Emalie thought. Oliver saw it, too. Lythia had already tipped her hand. "You want to save your brother. That's what you've been up to," Oliver said. And shockingly, that was just like what Bane had done for him.

"Ta-dah!" Lythia thrust her finger in the air. "All that time with humans and zombies hasn't completely dumbed you down, Nocturne. But don't think I'm telling you any more."

"Why are you telling us anything?" Oliver asked.

"Actually, that's a good question." Lythia's voice became strangely quiet. "I didn't want to," she said absently, "but you saw Alexy. Who tipped you off, anyway? Oh, wait . . ." Lythia rolled her eyes and walked away again. "Brotherhood. Got it. So, hey look, now you know that we have some things in common. But, Oliver, you know why villains usually tell their enemies everything, don't you?"

She bent down in the shadows on the far end of the boat. There was a scraping of metal. "It's mostly because we like to hear ourselves talk, but it's also because it's safe, telling our secrets to someone right before we slay them." She turned back around, and marched toward them holding a large battle-ax. "Well, Oliver Nocturne . . ." Her eyes gleamed.

"Wait—" Oliver stammered.

"Dean!" Emalie shouted hoarsely. Dean only watched silently.

Lythia swung the ax with lethal force. It passed within inches of Oliver's face, and sliced apart his chains before impaling in the planks of the deck.

"You are not my enemy," Lythia finished. "And I'm not your villain." She held out a hand to him.

Oliver couldn't hide the surprise on his face. He reached for Lythia's hand, and she helped him up.

Then promptly threw him off the boat. Oliver crashed into the water. He scrambled to the surface in time to see Emalie plunging in beside him.

Lythia leered down at them, dramatically wiping her hands clean. "You may not be my enemy, but you are a nuisance. And this whole thing with you and humans . . . *ick*. So hear this, Nocturne and Nocturne's blood bag: I don't care what you do. Leave town, go to the Darkling Ball together for all I care, but when the time for the Anointment comes, stay out of my way." She rummaged into her pocket and produced a tiny, red stone box. Oliver knew it all too well. "Stay out of my way, and your brother won't have been torched in vain," she said, waving the box containing Bane's ashes. "Come along, minions."

Lythia collapsed into a plume of smoke and snaked up into the night. Dean turned and followed the other zombies off the boat without so much as a glance at his soaked friends. They ran down the dock and across the parking lot, disappearing into the dark.

Oliver and Emalie swam to the boat's ladder, dragging themselves out of the frigid water. "Come on," said Oliver, seeing Emalie shivering in the cool ocean breeze. He tore open the door to the boat's cabin. He searched in the dark, through the cramped bedroom, finally finding a set of thick towels.

He turned and bumped right into Emalie. There was barely any room in the narrow space. Their eyes locked again, in that terrifying way that they had during basketball. Oliver had that feeling once again of being weightless in his own head, but he managed to turn his gaze away. He wrapped a heavy towel around her, rubbing her arms a few times for warmth.

"Thanks," said Emalie quietly.

"Mmm," Oliver replied. He tried to slip past her, but she grabbed his arm.

"Sit." He did. Emalie sat on the bed beside him, another shiver overwhelming her. "I want to dry off a bit. Let's go to the tree house."

"Okay," said Oliver.

They sank downward, until the foggy treetop appeared. It was nearing dawn now. The rim of gray sky was edged with pink. More birds called. The fire had died down to gray embers.

"Hey, guys." They both turned to find Dean sitting there. "What took you so long?"

"Dean," said Emalie in relief, "but your necklace . . ."

"Yeah, I know, bummer." Dean frowned. "But this place is beyond Lythia's control. I must still be my own person, at least a little bit, when she's controlling me."

Oliver smiled, relieved. And then he understood more. "Wait, does this mean . . ."

Dean grinned. "Yep. I can tell you what Lythia is up to."

"I believe her," Emalie said quietly.

"Lythia?" Oliver asked. "Yeah, well, me, too. I don't know what to make of it."

"She's going to try to save her brother," said Emalie. "But you don't think she wants to undo the prophecy, do you?"

"No," Oliver agreed. "Maybe she wants to get Anointed in her brother's place."

"But she's got a demon already," said Emalie. "The prophecy says it has to be a demonless vampire."

"Maybe she has a way to remove her demon," Dean mused.

"Can that be done?" Emalie asked.

"I've never heard of it," said Oliver, "but, anything's possible if she has Désirée's help." Something else occurred to him. "That's why she needed Bane's ashes."

"What would those do?"

"Well, Bane's ashes would still have his specific force signatures. He and I, and Alexy, had to be created a certain way to exist without demons in us, even though we were sired. Lythia would need to alter herself in the same way. Having Bane's ashes would be like having the code to that."

"And Désirée could make that happen," Emalie added. "Lythia gets Anointed in Alexy's place, and then she'd be the vampire to open the Gate."

"And if she gets Anointed," Oliver continued, "the prophecy can't be undone."

"But even if Dean knows where she is, how are we going to stop her? We can't slay her."

"Yeah, please don't," said Dean, as slaying Lythia would also destroy her minions.

"And we can't just stop Lythia," said Emalie, " 'cause then Alexy could still be Anointed. Or you."

"So we need to stop the Anointment altogether," said Dean.

"But how?" Oliver wondered. "Vyette is gonna have big power, and Half-Light will be there with their Pyreth Guardians. We can't go up against them."

Emalie sighed. "You know who would know . . ."

Oliver nodded. "The Brotherhood. Braiden said to get in touch."

"And we still don't think that's a bad idea?" asked Dean.

"Who knows," said Oliver, "but they want to keep the Gate closed, and so do we."

"So how do we get in touch with him?" Emalie asked.

"I think there's only one way," said Oliver. "Dean, we'll be back."

Dean nodded. "Yeah, I'll just be here, and serving my master," he said with a frown.

Oliver and Emalie returned to the world and left the boat and the docks, Emalie still shivering. They found a pay phone by a locked-up snack bar.

Emalie dialed 9-1-1, then spoke in a low, throaty voice. "Detective Nick Pederson, please." She flashed a quick grin at Oliver. "Hi, Detective, this is Pauline, assistant to Emalie Watkins and Oliver Nocturne, the vampire," she said, like she was making an important business call. Sometimes Oliver couldn't believe her nerve. "Mmmhmm, right . . ."

She cupped the receiver. "He said he was expecting us. He's such a grouch." She spoke back into the phone. "Well, I sure *hope* you're tracing this call. . . . Your friend Braiden told my people to be in touch. We'd like to arrange a meeting immediately. . . . Mmmhmm, Ballard locks? Excellent. Thanks for your help as always!" She hung up, and Oliver heard Nick Pederson still talking as she did so.

"You're crazy," said Oliver.

"Just having a little fun before the world ends," said Emalie. "Come on."

✳

Oliver and Emalie made their way along a metal walkway, crossing a long canyon of black water. Here and there, a salmon jumped.

There were two locks, cavernous concrete halls whose water level would rise or fall to move ships between the Seattle lakes and Puget Sound. Beyond them, another catwalk paralleled an old dam. White tubes stuck out of the old concrete. Water shot from them, chutes for young salmon returning to the sea.

Braiden stood in the middle of the walkway. Oliver and Emalie approached invisibly, then popped into sight. Oliver peered toward the far shoreline suspiciously.

"Don't worry," said Braiden. "We have binoculars trained on you, but no stakes. So, I take it you saw the LeRoux boy."

"Yeah," said Oliver, annoyed by Braiden's smug tone.

"And now we need to stop the Anointment," Emalie added.

"That's not going to make Half-Light very happy," said Braiden. "Miss Lythia, either."

"Can you help us or not?" Oliver snapped.

Braiden smiled. "Of course I can. What did you have in mind?"

Oliver and Emalie had talked about it on the way. "We'll be no match for Vyette," said Oliver, "so our only chance is to destroy the Artifact before she's summoned."

"That was our assessment as well," said Braiden. "Well done, team Oliver." Braiden held out a thin, golden tube, the size of a large Magic Marker. Something rattled inside it. "This is a kunai scorpion. It can be controlled with a basic behavior enchantment. Should be no sweat for an Orani. And it will destroy the Artifact. But tell me this: How are you going to get to the Artifact? Half-Light has it under tight security until the Anointment."

"Well, that's simple," said Emalie confidently. "We'll be going to the Anointment. We have it all figured out."

We do? Oliver thought to her. This was news to him.

"Well, then I guess 'good luck' is in order," said Braiden. "You'll need it."

As he disappeared into the dark, Oliver turned to Emalie. "What —"

"Not here." She pulled his arm and led him back across the catwalks, into an arboretum that bordered the locks. They found a secluded spot among the tall trees and twisting grass lawns, then sat and returned to the tree house.

"How are we going to get into the Anointment?" Oliver asked immediately.

"You're going to the Anointment?" Dean asked. "Whoa, what did I miss?"

"Getting you in is easy," said Emalie. "You just go home and pretend you've had a change of heart. It's getting me in that's the tricky part, but I know a way."

"Emalie, we can't just sneak you in," said Oliver worriedly. "There'll be dead detectors, the Reader, Pyreths. Your disappearing trick, even Jenette's cloaking, it won't be enough."

Emalie smiled. "That's why we have to walk right through the front door."

"And how are we going to do that?"

"I'll be your date, silly!" said Emalie, again with that unnerving confidence. "Just like Lythia suggested."

"What?" Oliver stammered. "Did you hear what I just said —"

"Yeah," said Emalie, "I did. You can't get me in *alive*. But there are other ways."

"Emalie . . ." Dean groaned.

Emalie gazed seriously at Oliver. "I can be your vampire date."

"What?" Oliver exclaimed. "No! What are you talking about? You want me to *sire* you?"

Emalie rolled her eyes. "Not *really*. Yuck. I mean make it *look* like you did."

"But I — even if what you were saying wasn't crazy — I don't have a demon. I can't sire. No one would believe it."

"So we find a vampire who would. Who would *say* that he did."

"And then what?" asked Dean skeptically.

"Then we go to the Ball together and destroy the Artifact." Oliver stared hard at Emalie, feeling a deep worry at the excitement on her face. She met his gaze. "I know what you're thinking, and if you say 'no,' I'm just going to do it anyway."

Oliver realized that she would. And he could think of no other way to stop the Anointment. "Okay," he said warily. "Maybe I know a vampire who would help us. But how are we going to make you look sired?"

"If I tell you any more now, you'll just worry too much."

"I think we're both worrying too much already," offered Dean.

"Oliver, you know we have to do this."

Oliver didn't want to agree, but . . . Yes, they did. Stop the Anointment, and then go find his parents and undo the prophecy. If this was the only way, then . . .

"Trust me," said Emalie.

"Okay."

❖

"**O**liver," said Phlox, and Oliver thought he saw surprise in her eyes when he trudged into the kitchen just before dawn. "How was your night?"

"Fine," he said.

"What have you been up to?"

"Nothing, really." He went to the fridge and grabbed a Coke.

"Good morning, Son." Sebastian emerged from the living room. Tyrus and Leah were behind him. Sebastian shared a quick, concerned glance with Phlox before saying: "Nice to see you home."

"Where else would I go?" Oliver asked innocently.

"Hello, Oliver," said Tyrus.

"Hey," said Oliver casually, taking a gummified tapeworm from the jar on the counter.

"So," Phlox asked, "were you at school all night, tonight?"

Oliver looked from his parents to Tyrus and Leah. It had become so easy to see through the silence, after all these months of going around in circles. Tyrus and Leah were obviously here because Oliver had been missing.

And if Oliver hadn't come home by dawn, it would have been time to tell Phlox and Sebastian about Alexy. Maybe, at this point, that was even what Half-Light was hoping for.

And yet, instead, here was Oliver, home on time, saying honestly, "No, I actually left early." He tried to get his tone just right. "I was scared about the Anointment and I — I just wanted to be alone and think it through. It's such a big responsibility, and sometimes I don't want it. . . ."

"That's understandable," said Sebastian. He gave Tyrus and Leah a reassuring glance. "There's nothing wrong with a little doubt."

"But I realized that it's gonna be okay," Oliver continued. "It's like you've all been saying, I was made for this, and any other vampire would be lucky to be in my position." Then he thought to add the icing on the cake. "Oh, and I got a date."

Phlox's eyes widened. "You did? Who is it?"

Oliver smiled. "It's a surprise. I gotta get some sleep. See you in the evening," he said with a pleasant smile, and headed for bed, leaving the adults in stunned silence behind him.

Chapter 11

The Darkling Ball

*R*eady?

"No," said Oliver aloud. He wasn't ready for this, at all. He sat on a pillow, floating above the floor of the Merchynt Sylvix's shop, deep in the Yomi. Across from him, Emalie sat on a pillow as well. She wore a crimson velvet dress that began just below her shoulders. It was fitted through her waist, and flared into a wide skirt. Her hair had made a completely unbraided appearance, and was tied back in a complicated pile behind her head. This accentuated the fine lines from her ears to her chin, down her long neck. Her scarab necklace hung like a jewel at the center of a crown made by her delicate collarbones.

The sight of her caused Oliver to tug nervously at the vest of his black tuxedo, to adjust the hand-knotted bow tie that his dad had so carefully done, to reconsider the matching set of hawk's eye shirt buttons and talon cuff links, handed down from Sebastian's father. Were they too much? Too old? Too creepy?

"Oliver," Emalie huffed. "Stop making your no-face and trust me."

"I do," said Oliver, but she looked so alive. Oliver remembered what she'd said on her birthday. There were proms ahead for her, a wedding, all so soon by vampire time. And it wasn't just that Oliver wouldn't be there for those events. What if this incredibly risky plan didn't work?

Then the world will end, anyway, Emalie thought in his head. *And eww! I can't believe you're thinking of me getting married!*

"I just —" he stammered, " —What about . . ." Oliver glanced behind Emalie, to where Sylvix stood, arms folded, his face shrouded in a hood.

"Don't fret, Mr. Nocturne," he said in a deep, vibrating voice. "Once the price has been paid, my services are incorruptible. And Ms. Watkins's credit is in good standing."

"Okay, there's that again," said Oliver doubtfully. *What are you paying them?*

Don't worry about it.

Oliver turned to Sylvix, well aware that he could hear their thoughts. "Tell me what she paid you."

"Of course. It is public record, after all. Ms. Watkins paid in days of happiness."

"What?" Oliver exclaimed. He glared at Emalie. "No, take it back."

"Sorry, no refunds," said Sylvix mildly.

"Relax, it was only twelve days." Emalie flashed her confident smile, but it faded faster than usual.

Oliver couldn't believe this. Didn't Emalie understand how dangerous those days of pure unhappiness would be? "Did you at least get to pick which days?" he asked worriedly.

"Oliver, stop. And no. Self-selected days weren't as valuable."

Oliver rolled his eyes. Of course they weren't! Nothing was as valuable in the demon world as stolen joy, especially because of the danger it posed to the victim. What if Sylvix took a happy day when Emalie needed one most?

It's done. Just take my hands and forget about it.

"Fine." Oliver grasped her hands. They were cold and clammy.

"Now keep me still." Emalie turned to Sylvix. "Ready."

Just then the lights went out. There was a moment of darkness, and then Sylvix's shop was lit in red. As they regularly did in the Yomi, directions and gravity had shifted. Sideways was now upside down. Emalie and Oliver were unaffected, sitting on their floating pillows. The Yomi's air horn sounded, and huge gears began to grind. The ladders and shops readjusted, shelves realigning around them.

Sylvix bustled among his wares. When he returned, he held a thin brass lancet with a razor-sharp tip. It was attached to a rubber hose, which snaked to Sylvix's other hand, where he held a white plastic milk jug.

Oliver frowned. "You're going to put it in that?"

Sylvix's eyes glowed a touch brighter. "Recycling is important," he said seriously. "And it's the perfect size. I used to use Narakan obsidian jars, but they shattered too easily. Now, Ms. Watkins, you will feel a slight sting."

Sylvix plunged the lancet into Emalie's neck, just above her shoulder.

Emalie's eyes bulged, her mouth scrunching as she tried to keep from crying out. Her fingers dug into Oliver's hands, her body trembling.

"Hang on, Emalie," Oliver said as supportively as he could. Her gaze locked with his. Meanwhile, Oliver was overcome by a woozy feeling as the tangy scent of her blood washed over him.

There was a splattering sound, as the milk jug began to fill, pump by pump.

"Small coincidence, don't you think, Mr. Nocturne," Sylvix said matter-of-factly, "that humans prefer the gallon as the optimum amount of liquid to carry around, when it's nearly exactly how much blood is in each of their bodies. I find subtleties like that amusing."

"Right," muttered Oliver. He tried to ignore the scent of Emalie's blood, the sound of it leaping free from her carotid artery. A single drop of it ran slowly along the lancet's shaft.

"Monterey," Emalie said absently, her voice little more than a whisper. Her gaze was still locked on Oliver, but had become distant. A tear gathered beneath her right eye.

"What?" Oliver asked.

"Mom and Dad took me to the beach. . . . I wished I had a camera for the cliffs. . . . Then they gave me the old one for Christmas. . . . No, don't go. . . ." Her head slumped to her chest.

The sucking sound quieted, the flow slowing to a drip in the milk jug.

"Just about empty," said Sylvix, sounding satisfied.

Oliver watched, horrified, as Emalie's skin paled to a bluish gray, and then light began to form just above her head. A beautiful white, sparking with blue edges . . . lifting away from her.

Oliver looked down at Emalie's cold, gray hands, and read the words he'd scribbled on the back of his hand for just this moment:

"*Revelethh . . . lucenthh . . . persechhh . . .*"

Nathan appeared beside Oliver. *Hey*, he said, then

reached out and took Emalie's soul by its hand as it rose from her body, looking around blankly. *You can stay with me*, he said to it.

"You'll take it to the Shoals," said Oliver.

Yes. She'll be safe, I promise.

Okay. See you when we're done. Oliver watched worriedly as the two souls winked away.

He turned to find Emalie staring vacantly at him. "Hey," she said flatly.

"Hey." Oliver turned to Sylvix. "It worked?"

"Of course," Sylvix replied. "She is dead, yet not."

"I don't feel so good," said Emalie blankly.

Sylvix thoughtfully reached over and dabbed away the last bits of blood by the wound in Emalie's neck. Then he put down the rag and the tip of his finger ignited in flame. He held it to Emalie's skin and burned a second black hole beside the lancet wound, making it look as if vampire teeth had done this work.

Oliver looked down at the milk carton, swaying heavily in his hand. "You're gonna keep that safe?"

"Of course, Mr. Nocturne. When Emalie requires it, I shall deliver it."

"What about a demon presence?" Oliver asked. "To make her seem like a vampire?"

"Oh, she does not require one," said Sylvix. "There is already a demon presence attached to her. See for yourself."

Oliver looked again at Emalie, reaching out for the forces, and suddenly felt a strong, prickly sensation from Emalie. It overwhelmed him, so similar to how it felt to be around Lythia, and yet this was much more familiar. Almost as if he'd known this demon presence for a long time. Had Emalie had some kind of demon within her all along? Was that what allowed her to converse with the dead? Or, was this the essence of her Orani nature, free to reach the surface?

"I have never before encountered something like this in a human," said Sylvix. "It is indeed a dark portent."

"What do you mean?" Oliver asked worriedly.

"I mean what I say. Now I believe you have a ball to attend."

"Let's go, Oliver." Emalie had gotten to her feet and was wobbling slightly.

You sure you're up to it? Oliver thought, but Emalie didn't reply. Their mental connection had been lost now that she was undead. "Okay," he said aloud, and stood and took her by the arm, leading her toward the door.

As they left Sylvix's, Emalie paused, gazing over the chasm. "Lots of death around," she murmured, then started up the ladders.

They climbed out of the Yomi, and passed through the nearly empty Underground Center, to the first gap between the levels. Emalie's skin remained pale and blue, but a slight fire had returned to her eyes. "I'm feeling a little better," she said.

"Good," said Oliver.

She glanced around. "There are so many forces," she said in amazement. "Everywhere. Pulling in every direction."

"Yeah," Oliver agreed, but it sounded like Emalie was feeling them even more strongly than he did.

"Don't you just want to fly away?" Emalie lifted off the ground and easily floated upward, without disappearing.

"Emalie," Oliver began, but then watched in shock as she effortlessly ascended all the way to the top floor. Not even a year ago, he'd had to carry her on his back from floor to floor. Now he was trying to keep up, but with his beginner's skill at levitation, he had to stop on each level to refocus and grab the forces again. On the second level from the top, he cast a cautious look toward Désirée's. The shop was dark.

Emalie was waiting for him by the silent food court. Its chairs were overturned and placed on top of tables. She reached out and jabbed him in the chest with her finger. "Slowpoke," she said playfully, then turned in a whirl of dress, and started off.

"These stores kinda grossed me out," she said casually as they crossed the top level. She paused to look over leather-clad mannequins in one shop window. "But now I get it. Who'd want to dress like a boring old human when you could feel things like this?" She gazed around again, almost like she could *see* the forces.

"I guess," said Oliver, wondering if he preferred the grossed-out Emalie, who used to cling tightly to his sweatshirt in this place.

They left the Underground and proceeded through the sewer tunnels. As they did so, Oliver slipped back to the tree house. It was daytime in the Delta. Emalie was there, but she sat perfectly still, eyes closed.

"How's it going?" Dean asked. He glanced warily at the unresponsive Emalie.

"Fine," mumbled Oliver, not wanting to get into it. "Where are you guys at?"

"We just left the Vera Project," Dean reported. "Lythia was hungry. . . . Pretty good bands, though. It was one of those Three Imaginary Girls shows. Have you ever heard —"

"Dean," Oliver said sharply.

"Right, sorry. We're downtown now. In the sewers beneath Fifth Avenue. Looks like we're headed for the Ball."

Oliver nodded. "Okay, well, we're almost there, too. Keep me posted."

"Roger that," said Dean.

Oliver drifted back up to the world. He and Emalie soon reached a set of glass double doors in the sewer wall. Frosted letters across the doors read: INIQUITY BANK TOWER. "Here we are," he said nervously. He stepped forward and the doors slid open automatically. It all came down to these next few steps.

As they crossed the threshold, they passed through an invisible, liquidlike wall: a dead detector. Emalie stepped right through it, then shrugged nonchalantly. "No problem," she said.

"There's more," said Oliver, flustered. Ahead, standing before gold elevator doors, was the black-cloaked Reader, its single eye glowing. "Just act like you belong," said Oliver.

"Mmm," said Emalie. She reached over and took his hand with her cold fingers.

The Reader stared at them as they approached. Oliver nodded to it. "Hi," he said. They reached the elevator, Oliver pressed the up arrow, and they waited. The Reader looked them over. There was a ding and the elevator doors opened. Oliver and Emalie stepped in. Turning, Oliver found the Reader watching them, but not reacting.

"*Ciao*," said Emalie. Oliver turned to see her smiling with feigned charm. The doors slid closed.

"Emalie, careful," Oliver warned. "It's only going to get harder."

"Just watch me," Emalie murmured.

The elevator rocketed upward, and the doors opened

onto an enormous hall carved from the top five floors of the tower. The Darkling Ball was in full swing. The focal point of the room was a wide wooden dance floor at the base of a large orchestra stage. The floor was consumed in a flurry of spinning tuxedoes and dresses. Couples mingled around the perimeter, holding crystal goblets, laughing and chatting. Groups watched the dancers from the many balconies above.

"Oliver?" Phlox and Sebastian approached. Sebastian wore a tuxedo with long tails, and Phlox was wrapped in a ruffled purple gown.

Time to play the part, Oliver thought nervously to Emalie, but then remembered that she couldn't hear him. He smiled at his parents. "Hey, guys," he said, and watched as Phlox and Sebastian surveyed Emalie in awe, noting the bite marks, the bluish skin, and sensing her mysterious demon presence.

"Oliver," Phlox repeated, her eyes wide. "Is she . . ."

"I needed a date for the ball," said Oliver, trying to sound nonchalant.

Others were gathering now. Tyrus, Leah, even Seth and his parents.

Sebastian peered at Emalie. "But, Oliver, how did you do this?"

Right on cue, a voice spoke from behind them. "I helped." Everyone turned to see Ty Gimble, Bane's old friend, leaning against the wall by the elevator. "Little

Nocturne said he'd found a date, but he needed help *asking* her." Ty grinned. "It was the least I could do for my friend's younger brother."

"We never thought . . ." said Phlox, fighting a smile, "this is . . ."

"Extraordinary," said Sebastian, clapping Oliver on the shoulder. "Hello, Emalie, I'm —"

"Call me Syren," said Emalie, extending her hand.

What are you doing? Oliver thought frantically, but once again, there was no reply. Giving herself a vampire name? Emalie was taking this too far, but Oliver had no choice now other than to smile and play along. "Thanks again, Ty," he said.

"No prob, always glad to help." Ty licked his teeth and sauntered off proudly.

"Well then," said Phlox, "I — I'm just stunned." She glanced up to the arched glass ceiling high above. Spanning the windows was a gold band with discs, tracing the path that the moon would take on the equinox. When it reached the exact middle, it would be time for the Anointment. The moon was more than halfway there. "There's still a little time. Have fun."

"Thanks," said Oliver. He led Emalie away from the crowd, feeling their amazed eyes on him. The problem child had made good. Everyone seemed convinced. And Ty had played his part perfectly. Still, Oliver had no idea what to make of his date.

"What were you doing making up a vampire name? Are you crazy?"

"Relax," Emalie scoffed. "They totally bought it."

They reached the tables of refreshments by the walls. There was a line of cooks holding fry pans over a trough of magmalight, frying up night crawlers in agave nectar. Beyond them was a lavish table of desserts, featuring sparkling crystal sculptures made entirely of hard candy. An attendant used a small blowtorch to remove pieces of the sculptures for guests to suck on.

"You want a worm?" asked Oliver. "After those chocolate cockroaches, these are easy."

"How about we have some of that?" Emalie said with a mischievous smile, glancing over to where the drinks were being served.

There was an elaborate fountain made of glass and silver. Crimson liquid cascaded down the levels, ending in crystal punch bowls at the base. The fountain was fed by a line of brass nozzles. Copper pipes connected these to cages hanging down from the ceiling on chains. Each cage was long and thin, made of black metal, and held an upside-down human. They were in Staesys, frozen in time, unaware that their blood was being drained.

"Emalie —" Oliver began.

"It's Syren," she said, a devilish smile on her face.

"Come on," Oliver said, flustered. "*I* can't even have that stuff. Can you try to remember that you're not really a vampire?"

"Why?" said Emalie. "Everybody here thinks I am. Why not have some fun?"

"You're just —" Oliver stammered "— It shouldn't be *fun* for you."

Emalie rolled her eyes. "You're being boring."

"No, I'm not," Oliver muttered.

"Okay, fine. No blood. Let's dance, then," said Emalie more quietly, finally sounding a bit like her living self.

Except dancing was terrifying. "Well . . ."

Emalie grabbed his arm and led the way out into the spinning couples. Oliver watched the other dancers and tried desperately to remember all the steps that he and every other vampire child were taught. . . . Yes, okay, they were doing Karloff's fox-trot, which was like the traditional box step dance, only with a quick, levitating half spin replacing the fourth step.

"Come on," Emalie said, grinning. "Sweep me off my feet."

"I —" Oliver had no idea what to say. He felt a new kind of awkward around her, but managed to take her hand and shoulder and ease them into the dance. They spiraled among the couples, Oliver working overtime not to mess up the steps, or crush Emalie's toes.

But it went pretty well. Oliver was fairly musical, and he'd been a quick study of the formal dances in school, which had of course earned him lots of taunting from Bane. *Who knew little lambs could dance?*

They passed Theo and Kym on the floor, both of whom gaped at Oliver and his date. He saw Phlox and Sebastian among the dancers, smiling in his direction, and Oliver did his best to smile back. It seemed that they really had pulled this off.

"It's funny," said Emalie.

Oliver reeled in his gaze and found her mere inches from his face again. She had pulled in close enough that their bodies were just touching. "What's funny?" he gasped.

"It's funny how you don't breathe," she said, and put her head against his shoulder. Oliver thought he might melt. The weight of her against him, the ruffling of her dress against his jacket. "You're so still, except when you speak, but then, still again."

"You're not breathing, either," said Oliver.

"Yeah, I know. It's so much more *calm* when you don't have to suck in air all the time."

"I guess," Oliver agreed, and yet, he bristled at hearing Emalie talking about her undead condition with such *interest*. Then again, her soul was out of her body. . . . Maybe it wasn't strange at all. But Oliver missed the living Emalie, who would have been conflicted: thinking the danger of this was interesting, but also being just slightly turned off and worried by . . . well . . . the vampire-ness of it.

"It's too bad we couldn't be like this all the time," Emalie said.

"What?" Oliver leaned back from her.

Emalie fixed him with a deadly serious gaze. Her eyes seemed to grow two sizes bigger, her dark brown pupils suspended in those strangely clear whites. "Come on, admit it. What's the point of living if you're just going to die? It's such a *waste*. And it comes so *soon* for a human. Besides . . ." The corner of her mouth rose in a mischievous grin.

Oliver only managed to make a confused face. "Besides what?" he croaked.

"Well, you *like* me, don't you?"

"I —" Oliver had the urge to say, *Duh!* Of course he liked her! But she wasn't supposed to *ask* him about it! In the thousands of times that Oliver had nervously imagined a moment like this between himself and Emalie, a moment when Oliver might really *say* something to her that captured the way he felt about her all the time, when they might even *kiss* . . . It wasn't like this.

"Come on, Oliver," Emalie said again, almost like it

was a dare. "It's better having me dead, isn't it? We'd never have to grow apart."

Oliver felt a rushing, like everything inside him was being swept away, leaving a hollow space. Here they were, dancing, together, and who knew if there'd be a moment like this for them ever again? But if she were like him, there could be. She could even join him if he opened the Gate. They could explore the higher worlds forever.

"It could be fun," Emalie whispered, and Oliver found her leaning toward him. Oliver began to lean in as well. Her black-hole eyes seemed to grow beyond a logical size, sucking him inward, her lips *right* there, bluish purple against her gray-and-lavender skin. . . .

But it wasn't right. Oliver pulled back until they were at arm's length. "Let's get some punch," he said, leading her off the dance floor.

"Oliver," Emalie groaned as they reached the cascading fountain. Beside it was a simple glass bowl for the kids, advertised as Primate Punch.

"Sorry," he said, avoiding her eyes and focusing instead on filling a goblet.

"Ugh," Emalie huffed. "Sometimes you're such a lamb."

Oliver recoiled. "Don't call me that." He'd never imagined that word, *Bane's* word, coming from Emalie's mouth. "Everything's different with you like this, so

< 154 >

don't . . . Let's just get this over with and bring you back to life."

Emalie frowned and rolled her eyes, almost like Suzyn or another of his vampire classmates would. "Fine," she grumbled.

Oliver slugged back his drink. He went to refill his glass, when an arm fell across his shoulder.

"Oliver." It was Phlox, Sebastian beside her. Their faces were tight, nervous. "It's time."

Oliver glanced to the ceiling and saw the moon nearing the apex. He nodded, feeling a rush of nerves, and had that old urge to run, to escape, but it was far too late for that. "Emalie can come, right?" he asked. "It's important to me."

"Well, I —" Sebastian began, but stopped when Phlox gave him a severe look.

"Of course you can, Syren," Phlox said to Emalie. "You're a lucky girl to join us on a night as important as this."

"Thank you," said Emalie.

They crossed the room. Around them, the party swirled on, but here and there, figures were beginning to move toward a set of inconspicuous black metal doors at the back of the hall.

The Nocturnes arrived just after the doors slid closed, taking an elevator full of Half-Light's innermost circle down to the site of the Anointment. Two Pyreth

Guardians stood on either side of the doors. They were hunched, lizardlike creatures with magma-colored eyes. Their skin looked like it had been burned to a crisp. It was sectioned into large, charred plates, and the spaces between glowed like molten rock.

"Hey, Seb." The Nocturnes turned to see Tyrus and Leah behind them.

"Hello, Tyrus," said Sebastian, his tone businesslike. "Well, after all the worries and second-guessing, here we are."

There was a humming as the elevator returned, and the black doors slid open. Sebastian started forward, but the Pyreths stepped into his path.

Sebastian nodded to the Guardians. "Let us pass, please."

They didn't move.

"Listen, Seb," said Tyrus awkwardly, "there's been a change of plans."

Phlox frowned at the guards. "We're not going down," she growled, "are we?"

"I'm afraid not," said Tyrus. "Ravonovich wants to see you first."

"But —" Phlox began, her voice rising.

Leah took her by the arm. "You know better than to make a scene."

"By all means," said Sebastian quietly, his jaw clenched.

"Come on, everyone," said Tyrus, moving toward a nearby hallway.

"What's going on?" Oliver asked.

Phlox put her arm around Oliver's shoulder. "It's okay, Oliver," she said.

But Oliver understood that it wasn't.

CHAPTER 12

The Last Betrayal

Oliver, Emalie, Phlox, and Sebastian were marched through a labyrinth of finely appointed halls, the pleasant music and revelry of the Ball fading behind them. Tyrus and Leah were in the lead, the Pyreths in back. Their footsteps were silent on deep burgundy carpet.

Tyrus opened a set of dark-wooded doors and they entered an expansive office. The entire back wall was a window looking out on the night skyline.

"Good evening, Nocturnes." Ravonovich stood behind a wide desk, his back to them, gazing out the window.

"What's going on?" Sebastian demanded angrily.

Ravonovich turned, a grin revealing his jagged, parchment-colored teeth. "Mind your tone, Sebastian," he said calmly. "What's going on, indeed. Why don't you ask your boy?"

< 158 >

"What's that supposed to mean?" asked Sebastian.

Ravonovich's eyes bore into Oliver. "Where to even begin . . . How about with why he was at the bus station last night? Where were you headed, Oliver?"

"Oliver, what is he talking about?" Phlox asked.

"Yes," Ravonovich continued, "our boy Oliver was picking up right where his traitor brother left off. Bane's treachery is now yours, isn't that right? Where were you going?"

"Bane's . . ." Phlox began. "Oliver, what were you trying to do?"

Oliver scrambled to think of what to say, something that would be truthful enough to satisfy them without revealing everything. "I — it's the same as I told you," said Oliver, "I was having doubts about the prophecy. . . ."

"Sure you were." Ravonovich smiled again. "And then you thought it over and decided that, contrary to everything you've done in this last year, you'd just kill your human friend and fulfill the prophecy after all, is that it?"

"I . . . yeah," said Oliver, understanding how pathetic it sounded.

"I think you've failed to mention a few important facts, haven't you, boy?"

"I don't know —" Oliver began.

< 159 >

Ravonovich talked right over him. "For example, that your girlfriend hasn't been sired at all. The enchantments may have fooled the party — and your parents, who are so desperate to believe in you — but they don't fool me. You and your Orani are here for a far different purpose."

"That's ludicrous," Sebastian argued.

"Is it?" said Ravonovich. "Well, there's more. Yasmin," he called. By the wall, Yasmin flicked on a television screen, and there were Oliver and Emalie, standing with Braiden Lang at the locks.

"They've plotted with our most dire enemies," said Ravonovich, "and come here tonight to destroy the Artifact."

"That's nonsense —" Phlox protested.

"Check her bag," ordered Ravonovich.

Tyrus stepped dutifully over to Emalie and took her purse. Emalie didn't protest. He rooted inside and produced the brass cylinder.

"A kunai scorpion," said Ravonovich, "given to them by the Brotherhood."

"Oliver," Phlox gasped, eyes wide.

"And oh, no, it doesn't end there," said Ravonovich. "Oliver has been in contact with Bane's treachery."

Sebastian spoke quietly now, staring at the floor. "You still haven't told us —"

Ravonovich's mouth curled in distaste. "Oliver has found his human soul."

"What?" Phlox asked, horrified.

"Yes, Oliver's soul lingers in the world, and Bane's treachery was to summon it. Oliver was planning to flee with his soul, to *merge* with it, in an attempt to undo the prophecy."

"Tsss," Phlox hissed. Oliver couldn't believe the shame and disgust in that sound.

"Oh, yes," said Ravonovich. "And there's even more. They were headed to the home of his *human* parents, who somehow remain alive."

"Is this true, Oliver?" asked Sebastian, his voice flat, his eyes cold.

"It doesn't matter!" Oliver shouted desperately. "Ask him why we're not downstairs right now!"

"I think, in light of the evidence, that's obvious," Ravonovich hissed.

"They have a backup plan!" Oliver shouted. "Alexy LeRoux. They've been prepping him since the start. They've been lying to us! I was never the last chance."

Sebastian and Phlox stared at him for a moment, their gazes hard, and both of them looked suddenly weary. Sebastian turned slowly to Ravonovich. "Is this true?"

Ravonovich chuckled. "Of course it's true! Don't kid yourselves. Do you really think, after all of Oliver's issues, all of your family's *failings*, that we would entrust our fate solely with him?"

Phlox's eyes glowed severely. "No, of course not."

"As well you shouldn't . . . Tonight will be a great night for the *vampyr*. The Anointment will proceed, but not with Oliver Nocturne."

"So then, what will become of him?" Phlox asked, her eyes smoldering, her face tight.

"I'm afraid you know the only course of action that remains," said Ravonovich icily. "Half-Light has tried everything in its power, spared no expense, to save Oliver Nocturne. Maybe it was the force treatments. . . . Perhaps they lowered Oliver's defenses, made him susceptible to the irrationalities of Finity. It is so much like a virus, after all. . . . But nonetheless, we have done everything we could, even protected him from his own brother, and yet the boy only becomes more of a danger to everything we have worked for. Alexy will be Anointed in his place."

"We should take Oliver home, then," said Phlox quietly.

"I'm afraid not," growled Ravonovich. "There can only be one demonless vampire child. Bane was old enough for us to put a demon in him, which allowed the prophecy to pass to Oliver. But Oliver is still too young for us to do the same, to pass it on to Alexy. And besides, what would the community think of such lenient treatment of a traitor?"

"What are you saying?" Sebastian asked quietly.

"Phloxiana, Sebastian, it is time for you to be free of this burden. To move on from this disappointing chapter," said Ravonovich sympathetically. "As I said before, Half-Light recognizes your sacrifices, your struggles, and you will be taken care of. We can help you find a human teen to sire, so that you might at least have a normal family from now until the Ascension. But first let's put this failure to rest. . . . Leah!"

Leah grabbed Oliver with an arm around his throat. She spun and backed up against Ravonovich's desk, facing Phlox, Sebastian, and Emalie.

"No!" Emalie lunged forward but Yasmin grabbed her in a similar hold.

"Wait!" shouted Oliver. "Mom, Dad!"

Phlox and Sebastian stared at him, their eyes glowing. "You deceived us," said Phlox quietly.

"There, there," said Ravonovich. "Worry not, Phloxiana. This will all be over in a moment."

"Please," Oliver gasped.

"The case of Oliver Nocturne is closed," said Ravonovich. "Tyrus . . ."

Tyrus brushed past Sebastian and Phlox, holding a long sword made of wood. "Sorry, Seb," he muttered.

"Mom, Dad," Oliver croaked. Their faces remained cold.

Then Sebastian grabbed Tyrus's shoulder. "I'll do it," he growled, taking the slaying sword. He stepped toward Oliver. "All that we endured," he hissed, "for nothing."

Oliver struggled against Leah's arm, his feet slipping on the floor. It couldn't end like this!

Sebastian's shadow fell over him and he stopped. Oliver gazed up into his father's narrowed, amber-glowing eyes. His face was twisted, grimacing, as if this thing below him was his greatest shame.

Oliver remembered his dad's words in Morosia, when he'd worried his parents might slay him for seventh moon. *Oliver, we would never.* But they had come a long way since then. And maybe tonight, Oliver had finally proved to them that he was beyond saving, that he was truly a failure.

"Good-bye," said Sebastian thickly. He raised the wooden sword.

Phlox threw a hand over her eyes and sunk away toward the wall.

Oliver wanted to cry out, to plead, but his voice was gone, his brain frozen. He thought of Nathan . . . of the parents he would never meet.

Sebastian lunged forward with the blade.

Oliver couldn't scream, couldn't move. Looking away,

he found Emalie's face —and her wide, clear eyes were washed away in an explosion of dust.

"NO!"

The colors of the world began to fade. Emalie became a silhouette in gray and white, and the world dissolved into static. Oliver felt himself falling backward, dust all around him. *Into the drift*, he had time to think —

Then he hit the floor hard. Dust rained on top of him. Oliver wiped frantically at his stinging eyes. But he still had eyes. He still had hands to wipe them with. . . .

And there was no longer an arm around his neck.

Oliver scrambled to his feet to see Sebastian whirling, spinning the sword over his head, slashing at the attacking blur of Yasmin, who had a long Naginata fighting stick forming in her hands. She exploded into dust.

Just as Leah had, when Sebastian had slain her instead of his son.

"Honey, look out!" Phlox yelled. She was in the corner of the room, wrenching two ancient, steel katana swords free from a display of armor. Tyrus was rushing toward her, and in a flurry of gown she spun and delivered a powerful roundhouse kick. Tyrus hurtled backward, crashing through the giant window and toppling into the night.

Wind howled through the room.

Sebastian turned to see a Pyreth lunging, its skin cracking and beginning to radiate fire —

There was a blur of smoke and steel, and suddenly the Pyreth was flipping backward into the air, its lizard head flying free in a jet of flames. A column of smoke was re-forming behind it — Phlox, a sword gleaming in each hand.

"Here!" she shouted and tossed one into the air. Sebastian leaped upward, grabbing it, somersaulting and simultaneously evanescing into smoke. The second Pyreth barely had a moment to lunge at Phlox before Sebastian re-formed behind it. Their blades swung from opposite sides, cleaving the creature in two and clanging together in the middle. It crumbled to the ground as smoldering embers. Phlox and Sebastian gazed at one another, then turned to Oliver, both their eyes glowing more fiercely than ever before.

Oliver's eyes glowed back at them. He stared at his dust-covered, sword-wielding parents, and felt a rush inside that was . . . complicated. They had just forfeited everything for him, and it almost made him feel guilty, because he'd never really known that they would. But then again who knew what went on in the minds of these grown-ups?

"Well then."

Phlox and Sebastian glanced behind Oliver, and the light in their eyes faded. Oliver jumped to his feet, spinning to find Ravonovich backed against the windows, with a dagger to Emalie's throat. "We'll just slay you all.

It's not a problem. I can see now that, just like your son, your minds have been corrupted by this miserable Finity." Ravonovich's hand snapped back.

"No!" Oliver shouted.

The blade plunged, but halted. Ravonovich stiffened as the glass splintered and cracked behind him. Suddenly he fell forward, atop Emalie. She hit the floor, but Ravonovich never did, his body dissolving into silver dust. A wooden stake clattered to the ground.

Oliver saw the stake-size hole in the glass. Smoke poured through it, and Tyrus reappeared.

"Tyrus, thank you," said Sebastian.

"Don't mention it," said Tyrus, rubbing his temple where Phlox's heel had left a gash. He looked at her sorely. "I was coming over to say that I'd help."

"Sorry," said Phlox, "just being cautious."

Oliver helped Emalie to her feet. "You okay?" he asked.

"Peachy," Emalie muttered. She looked down at the ash on the floor, and stamped on the pile for good measure.

"Now what?" Tyrus asked.

Sebastian and Phlox looked to Oliver. "What next, Oliver?"

Even after what had just happened, Oliver hesitated. What would they think of what he had come here to do?

"Oliver," Phlox said, smiling tenderly. "It's okay."

"Well," said Oliver slowly, "Ravonovich was right. We came to destroy the Artifact, before they can summon Vyette." Despite what they had just done, Oliver had to wonder if his parents would really go against all that they believed in —

"We can take the service elevators," said Sebastian. "The Anointment is being held in the magmalight substation beneath the building, for security. This way." Tyrus and Phlox fell in step behind him, crossing Ravonovich's office.

"Come along, Oliver," said Phlox briskly, and swept out the door.

Oliver shook his head. "Wow," he said, looking to Emalie with a relieved smile.

But her gaze was vacant, staring down at the ash on the floor. "So easy to be dusty . . ." she mumbled.

Oliver grabbed her hand and pulled her along.

They twisted through the halls, music from the Ball reverberating in the distance, until they found Sebastian, Phlox, and Tyrus waiting for them in a tiny elevator. Oliver and Emalie crowded inside, and the elevator rushed downward. Oliver felt his ears popping at the descent. There were no numbers on the elevator, but Oliver knew the magmalight substation would be deep underground.

The doors opened on a narrow tunnel with a grated metal floor, its walls and ceiling made of rock. Strips of red magmalight lined the walls. Tyrus motioned with his hand and led them forward. The air was hot and thick with steam. There was a deep rumbling of machinery, vibrating the floor. They passed numerous intersections, rats and lizards scurrying at their feet. Soon, an open space appeared ahead. Tyrus stopped at a ladder just before it.

"We can watch from the catwalks around the monitoring station," he said. Phlox and Sebastian nodded in agreement. They started up the ladder one by one.

At the top was a solid steel door with a keypad, and a catwalk leading away through the rock to the right. Tyrus ducked, spectralized, and crept in that direction. Everyone else did the same, Emalie disappearing as well.

The catwalk turned a corner, running alongside the front of the control room, beneath large windows. Oliver risked a glance inside, and saw banks of dense computer machinery.

To his right was a giant, cylindrical cavern. In the center was an island of rock. A column of black metal scaffolding dropped down to it from the darkness above, holding an elevator. The island was ringed by a bottomless fissure, its depths obscured by steam. Emerging from this fissure and rising up the cavern walls were huge tubes of magmalight in every color of its fiery spectrum, from brilliant hot whites to cool maroons.

A crowd of black-robed, hooded figures stood on the plateau, facing a gold altar. Atop this stood Malcolm LeRoux, his hood back, holding a small gadget in his hands. To Malcolm's side, Alexy sat in his wheelchair.

Beside Alexy was a large, round mirror, angling upward from the floor. Oliver looked up and found other mirrors on the walls of the cavern. They were bouncing a white beam of moonlight all the way from the roof of the building. The light bounced off the mirror by Alexy, then off another curved mirror that hung suspended on ropes a few feet above Malcolm's head. The beam shot straight down from this mirror, creating a vertical stream of light that ended at a square of black rock in the center of the altar.

"The equinox is moments away," said Malcolm, reading from the device in his hands.

The moonbeam narrowed, becoming brighter, its strength growing.

Oliver touched his wrist, and sank back to the tree house. "Dean, where are you guys?"

"In passages, underground," Dean reported. "I think we're close. What's up with you?"

"Almost got slayed," said Oliver. "Parents saved me. It was crazy."

"Your vampire parents?" asked Dean.

"Yeah," said Oliver, and realized he hadn't thought about *which* parents he'd been referring to.

"Well, go do this thing, then," said Dean. "Before we get there."

"Right." Oliver returned to the world. This was it.

"Bring forth the Artifact," Malcolm instructed below.

Phlox, Sebastian, and Tyrus looked to Oliver. Oliver turned to Emalie. "Ready?"

But Emalie was looking around warily. "This place looks familiar. Like I've seen it before . . ."

"Emalie, get the scorpion out," Oliver whispered frantically.

Emalie shook her head. "Right." She removed the cylinder from her bag and twisted off the top. Reaching inside, she pulled out the flapping creature by its leathery wing, its stinger snapping in the air. It was small, with black batlike wings and a yellow segmented body. "Okay, ready."

"Here it comes," whispered Phlox, eyeing the side of the cavern.

Two Pyreth demons emerged from a tunnel, crossing a metal catwalk out onto the rock island. They carried a black cloaked form between them. It moved, walking like a person, its hands shackled. Oliver hadn't expected this. He'd just assumed that the Artifact was some mystical *object*.

"Blackness, afraid . . ." Emalie muttered faintly.

"What?" Oliver asked.

The Pyreths reached the altar and stood the figure directly below the suspended mirror, in the beam of moonlight.

"Now," said Oliver.

"Let the great Vyette be summoned," called Malcolm. He pulled the black cloak off the Artifact, revealing a head of long, braided brown hair and wide dark eyes, a woman in a long white gown. . . .

"Emalie, *now*!" Oliver hissed.

But instead, Emalie gasped. "Mom?"

CHAPTER 13

The Anointed

Oliver looked from Emalie to the Artifact. There was no doubt that it was Emalie's mother, Margaret.

"You missed your chance," Margaret said defiantly to the group below.

Malcolm smiled. "I think not. *Arrivethhh...*" Malcolm intoned.

Flares of colored light began to swirl around Margaret.

Emalie was shaking. "We have to get her," she said.

Oliver felt at a loss. He turned to Phlox. She was also glancing from Emalie to Margaret. "I take it we won't be killing the Artifact now," she said.

"We have to get her out," said Oliver.

"I don't think there's time for that anymore," said Phlox.

"*Salvethhh!*" Malcolm shouted.

The room was overwhelmed by a flash of light. For a moment, Oliver was frozen in place, and saw that everyone else was as well. The magmalight had stopped moving in its tubes.

A bright disc of light formed near the altar, and from it stepped a tall, thin woman with smooth charcoal skin and blazing sapphire eyes. Her white hair was wrapped high on her head, and she wore a white gown. Her black hands were clasped in front of her. She was the only moving thing in the room, striding to the center of the altar, to stand before Malcolm and Margaret.

"Hello, everyone," she said softly, and the room began to move again. They all stared silently at the higher being, Vyette, arrived from a distant world. She looked around the chamber. "Thank you for inviting me." She reached into her gown and removed a small, golden dagger. "Who is to be Anointed, and so become an instrument of the rebellion against the Architects?"

"This is the boy," said Malcolm, waving a hand to his son. "Alexy LeRoux, prepared according to the prophecy."

"I see," said Vyette. She looked kindly at Alexy, but shook her head. "He is lovely, but I'm afraid you're mistaken, vampire. This is not the one."

"What?" Malcolm stuttered. "I —"

"I'm sorry but I have quite a busy day," said Vyette pleasantly. "So I ask again, who is to be Anointed?"

"It's me," called a voice from across the cavern. Oliver turned to see Lythia marching in, Dean and her zombie minions behind her. Worried whispers passed among the crowd of hooded Half-Light vampires. Lythia led her zombies across the catwalk to the platform and pushed her way to the altar.

"Lythia?" Malcolm asked. "But you —"

"Relax, Dad," said Lythia. She looked to her brother. "Don't worry, Alexy, it's going to be fine."

"I'm sorry," said Vyette, smiling kindly at Lythia, "you are also not the one."

"That's what *you* think," said Lythia.

"Young one, I'm afraid I don't appreciate your tone," said Vyette.

"Tut-tut, Vyette," said another voice. "That's no way to speak to my protégé."

Vyette smiled, but her tone grew cold. "Why hello, Désirée."

Dead Désirée had appeared behind Vyette. "It's been awhile, dear."

A chorus of whispers rounded the room. Malcolm retreated behind Alexy's chair. Margaret teetered woozily, and backed away slightly as Désirée stepped to the altar.

"Now, Vyette," said Désirée, "I'm going to need you to Anoint the girl, and then you can be on your way." Her smile was constant, her white face pleasant, but now and then the skin seemed to bubble as the real face beneath it moved about.

Oliver was surprised to see a look of uncertainty cross Vyette's face, and he understood that Désirée was the most powerful being in the room.

"Désirée," said Vyette, "you know as well as I that she is not the one referred to by the prophecy."

Désirée's eyes melted into flat gold coins. "Yes, well," she said with a sigh, and flashed her hand at Vyette. "I never much cared for prophecies." A burst of red energy leaped from Désirée's fingers, slamming Vyette backward in an explosion of flames. She soared off the altar and fell out of sight into the steam-filled fissure.

The Anointing blade clattered to the floor. No one moved to oppose Désirée as she picked it up. She considered the blade, then gazed around the chamber. "Hello, vampires," she said theatrically. "You've always been kind to me — not that you had a choice — but I have appreciated how most of you let me run my shop and never did anything unwise such as question what I might really be up to. Others haven't been as smart, or as fortunate.

"Now, some of you know what I am and some of you don't. For those of you who do, you know that I'm really not supposed to be okay with your little scheme to open the Gate. A lot of hardworking beings put their hearts into that Gate, not to mention all the worlds that are held together because of it. I've been getting calls nearly every century asking me to stop you all.

"Thing is," Désirée continued, "I've come to a different opinion than my peers about the state of things. So guess what? You'll get your Gate opened. It's just going to be Lythia here that's going to do it. She's really the only one who can be trusted to do the job right. Now, that's going to be okay with everyone, right?"

The room was silent in reply, except for Emalie, who whispered so that only Oliver could hear. "Slayed me . . ."

Oliver turned to her. "What?"

He glanced back and found Désirée gazing curiously up at the catwalk.

Honestly, Oliver, Désirée suddenly spoke into his mind, *I thought you'd be in Arizona by now.*

You lied to me, Oliver thought back.

Oh, Oliver, I told you long ago: I don't lie. Though I have been vague, I suppose. Tell you what, to make up for everything, I won't slay you in order to pass the prophecy on to Lythia. I know Ravonovich said it was necessary but really, how much did he ever know about anything? You'll get to spend the time you have left in this world with your friends. So that's something, right?

Désirée's smile widened, causing ripples in her skin. "Now then, Lythia, ready?"

"Yes," said Lythia, and Oliver thought that she sounded almost nervous.

"What are we going to do?" he whispered to Emalie.

Phlox placed a hand on his shoulder. "We'll be no match for Désirée."

"This will hurt just a bit," Désirée said below. Her gold eyes flashed. She made a fist just above Lythia's chest, as if she was grabbing something tightly. Then she began to pull.

A wind rose in the chamber, and now a shimmering silver form began to pull free of Lythia. It writhed in protest, trying to wrap itself around Lythia and dive back inside. Oliver saw claws, horns, fangs, and glowing red eyes. It was Lythia's *vampyr* demon.

"This is horrible," said Phlox, watching the *vampyr*'s removal in awe.

The demon slipped out. Désirée held it in her fist like a fish on string, then in one lightning motion, she lunged forward. Her face seemed to peel back, and a giant mouth of yellow, saberlike fangs lashed out, gobbling up Lythia's demon in a single bite. Then Désirée was simply standing there again. "Mmm," she said, puckering as if she'd eaten something tart. "That was a strong one."

Lythia staggered, her face blank. Oliver sensed a change in her, the demon presence gone.

"And now the box . . ." said Désirée.

Lythia, her hand shaking, produced the small red stone box of Bane's ashes. She flipped open the lid.

Désirée swept her hand over the box and a long trail of ashes flew out, following her fingers. She swirled her hand and the ashes arced in the air like she was twirling a ribbon.

"Whuu —" Emalie said quietly beside him. "Idiot?"

Oliver glanced at her. "What?"

Emalie lurched and reappeared in the room. Oliver reached to steady her. "I got it, lamb," Emalie muttered, but it no longer sounded like her.

Below, Dean and the zombies grabbed Margaret, pulling her from the moonbeam, and then guided Lythia into it. Désirée flashed her hand and the stream of Bane's ashes flew at Lythia, wrapping around her like a swarm of insects. The spirals began to glow in different colors, and Lythia began to shake.

They had been right, Oliver thought. Remove Lythia's demon, then strengthen her body for the Anointment by using the force signatures from Bane's ashes.

"Now," announced Désirée over the swirling wind, "let's celebrate the Waning Sun!" She raised the Anointing blade over Lythia's chest.

Oliver watched helplessly. In a moment, he would be free of his destiny, and yet the end of the world would be assured.

"Tsssss . . ." Oliver turned to see Emalie getting to her feet. Her eyes flashed open, her irises bloodred, her pupils white. She looked down at him, her body beginning to glow a blinding white. "Watch out, bro," she snapped at him, but her voice wasn't merely her own. It also sounded like — Oliver replayed what Emalie had just said. *I got it, bro . . . idiot?* Those were his brother's last words.

"Bane?" Oliver asked dumbly, looking at Emalie.

She turned, her eyes blindingly bright now, and smiled. When she spoke, it was Bane's voice. "It's payback time."

"Charles?" Phlox whispered.

"Hey, Mom," said Emalie. "One more thing to do." Emalie's voice became a shrill scream that drowned out the entire chamber. "DÉSIRÉE!"

Désirée halted, looking up along with the rest of the chamber. "Well now . . ." she said.

And a fluid silver form lunged out of Emalie, its red *vampyr* eyes glowing, its fangs bared. With a terrifying screech, it slammed into Désirée in an explosion of light. The Anointing blade flew from her hand. Bane's *vampyr* and Désirée spiraled up into the cavern in a furious blur of thrashing limbs and fangs, flames swirling around them.

Emalie slumped against Oliver. "That feels better," she said faintly.

"Emalie!" Margaret called from below.

Oliver gazed up in wonder. . . . Bane. Oliver thought back on Emalie's condition in the weeks since Bane's slaying, and what Sylvix had said tonight. There was already a demon presence inside her . . . Bane's *vampyr*. Emalie had merged with it before, when they'd fought the Nagual demon, and had even connected with it as far back as the museum in Fortuna. His *vampyr* demon should have been extinguished when he was slain, but instead, it seemed to have found a safe haven in Emalie. How was that even possible?

Phlox tugged Oliver's shoulder. "This is our chance to get the Artifact and get out."

"We should get Lythia, too," said Oliver, "before she's Anointed." He turned to Emalie. "Can you go?"

She nodded. "Give me a hand, 'kay?" she said weakly.

Oliver put an arm around Emalie's waist and leaped, along with Phlox, Sebastian, and Tyrus, down to the platform.

"You!" Malcolm shouted upon seeing them, but could say no more before Sebastian landed a fist to his temple, knocking him senseless. The rest of the Half-Light vampires were torn between watching the battle above, and the arrival of the Nocturnes. A few lunged, clouds of smoke forming weapons in their hands. Phlox, Sebastian, and Tyrus spun into battle.

"Oliver!" Dean shouted.

"Get Lythia!" Oliver said.

Dean grabbed his master, who was so dazed she didn't object.

"Emalie!" Margaret pushed free of the zombies, who were watching Lythia dazedly. She rushed to Oliver and Emalie. "Oh, honey." She wrapped Emalie in a hug, but immediately pulled back. "What's happened to you?"

"Just a little dead," Emalie mumbled.

Margaret gazed seriously at Oliver. "You're the chosen vampire," she said, and then glanced back at Emalie. "We need to go, right now. Emalie shouldn't be here. Can you undo these shackles?"

The shackles were made to hold a human, and Oliver quickly tore them apart. "Okay, now what?"

Margaret closed her eyes, concentrating. "I can get us out of here, I just need to locate my bag. I hid it right before Half-Light caught me. . . ."

"Where's everyone off to?" Vyette floated up from the chasm, her dress singed, her eyes glowing brighter than ever, and the Anointing blade in her hand once more. She landed in front of Oliver and Emalie. "There is still an Anointing to be done, and finally, the *one* has arrived."

Emalie gathered herself and stepped in front of Oliver. "No, I won't let you do this to him."

"Emalie!" Margaret shouted, her eyes popping open. She scrambled to her feet.

Vyette smiled. "Why, I never intended to." In a lightning motion, she plunged the blade into Emalie's chest.

"No!" Margaret screamed.

Emalie fell against Oliver and her mother, slumping to the ground, wincing in pain. Oliver dropped to his knees beside her. The blade was sunk to the hilt in her chest.

All around them, the fighting ceased. Phlox, Sebastian, Tyrus, and the Half-Light vampires turned and gaped at Emalie. Dean pushed his way to her side, dragging Lythia along.

"Good-bye, vampires," said Vyette kindly, "and best wishes." A disc of light flashed around her, and she was gone.

"Emalie, oh, Emalie, stay with me," Margaret mumbled, her voice shaking.

As Oliver, Dean, and the crowd of vampires watched, the blade began to glow, burning with golden light, and sinking fully into Emalie. Then it was gone. There was no hole in the dress, and no blood.

Oliver heard a voice muttering from the stunned crowd. "There will come a young demonless vampire . . ." He turned to see Malcolm on his knees, staring at Emalie and reciting the prophecy. "Who has garnered a power never before known among them...A power..."

"We have to get her out of here," urged Margaret, her voice shaking with panic.

"The Orani girl," Malcolm said, his voice rising, "*she* is the power that the prophecy speaks of! The power that Oliver has garnered. The Anointment has succeeded!"

Oliver stared at Emalie in disbelief. She was part of the prophecy? Did that mean that they were destined to open the Gate and destroy the world *together*?

"Excellent!" Désirée's voice boomed through the chamber. A ball of light crashed down onto the altar, smashing through the moon mirrors. Désirée stood, her hair unkempt, and black slashes torn across her face. Something yellow, like a horn, was protruding from her white scalp. She held Bane's *vampyr,* writhing in her hand.

"That felt good!" Bane's voice called triumphantly. "I did what I could, kids," he said —

And Désirée devoured him.

"Tsss!" Phlox lunged, but Sebastian grabbed her. All eyes turned to Désirée.

She smiled at Oliver and Emalie. "Oh, Oliver," she purred, "I'm such a fool. You brought the key to opening Nexia's Gate right into my shop and I couldn't see it. All these months I've wasted preparing this one —" she

< 184 >

waved a hand dismissively at Lythia, slumped on Dean's shoulder, "— but then again, this really did work out, didn't it? I guess I'll just gather up my things and be gone."

Désirée stepped toward Emalie and Oliver.

"No!" It was Malcolm, of all vampires, who moved between her and Oliver. The rest of the vampires, Phlox, Sebastian, and Tyrus included, stepped up beside him.

Désirée's smile only widened. "You don't really want to do this."

"You won't take our son," Phlox hissed.

Désirée sighed. "Clearly my little costume is losing its creepy charm. Maybe it's time you miserable beings met the real me." She reached up, grabbed the skin by her eye, and pulled. Her face tore free, along with her hair. Beneath was a black, horned creature with enormous saber teeth and apple-size gold coin eyes. Hands appeared on wiry black limbs and Désirée's entire human form was torn away like paper. What stood before them was a ten-legged being with sixteen arms. The eight fingers on each hand came to long, razorlike points.

"Oh, my," said Phlox breathlessly. "She's an Architect."

"*Tachesss!*" Malcolm shouted, and the vampires attacked. Désirée battled back, arms spinning.

Vampires were thrown in all directions, some dissolving into dust.

"Oliver!" Phlox, Sebastian, and Tyrus ducked out of the fight. "Now's our chance."

Oliver hoisted up Emalie. "Nnnn," she mumbled faintly.

Dean appeared beside them. "We don't need Lythia anymore, right? 'Cause I had a great time dropping her on her face."

The group had just started toward the catwalk when Désirée's hideous, true form landed before them, claws digging into the rock. "Why, Oliver, I hope you're not thinking of leaving me. You and your lovely Anointed girlfriend."

"Stay away from them," said Margaret, stepping in front of Oliver and Emalie. She now held her woven bag in her hand. "You should know better, Désirée."

Désirée's fanged mouth seemed to smile. "That's a bold statement coming from a meager being such as yourself."

"It's not just coming from me," said Margaret, and she pulled a diamond-shape hand mirror from her bag. Oliver recognized it from Margaret's statue in Italy. But it was also the shape of the mirror Désirée had on the wall of her shop.

"Stand back!" Margaret called. Her eyes melted into gold coins like Désirée's. She thrust the mirror before her, and a beam of blinding light burst forth. It was white, and yet gold, but there were other colors, too. Oliver heard a soft voice he hadn't heard in a long time: *See me clearly.*

It was the light of the Gate itself.

Désirée staggered back, her many arms flailing. Margaret held the mirror steady, and with her other hand reached back for Emalie's. *Everyone join hands,* Margaret commanded in Oliver's mind. Emalie grabbed his, and when he turned to Phlox he saw that she had heard the command, too. She took Sebastian's hand, who grabbed Tyrus, who grabbed Dean . . .

"Heed this warning!" Margaret shouted at Désirée, who cowered in the light of the Gate.

And then she and Oliver and the rest disappeared from the chamber.

< 187 >

CHAPTER 14

The Old Ghost

They arrived on a quiet street, lined with flat, single-story houses. Each had an orange tiled roof, white stucco walls, and flowering cacti in their front yards. The street was asleep except for the steady flicking of a lawn sprinkler. In the distance, the jagged line of mountains stood against a pale blue sky, their peaks painted pink with sunlight. A faint moon floated above, along with a few dawn stars.

Oliver saw Phlox, Sebastian, and Tyrus looking around uncertainly. "It's where they live," he said to them nervously.

"Your human parents?" Phlox asked.

Oliver nodded. He looked to Emalie, who was leaning against his shoulder, shuddering, her skin blue.

"We need to bring her back to life," said Oliver seriously. After that, he had no idea. What did it mean that Emalie had been Anointed? What did it mean that Vyette made it sound like Anointing Emalie was supposed to happen? Margaret had wanted to get her out of there, almost as if she'd known of the danger. Now Emalie was part of the prophecy . . . a prophecy that could no longer be undone.

"Yeah . . . that would be good," Emalie said weakly. "Sylvix?" she called.

"Pardon me." Oliver looked up to see Sylvix easing his way between Sebastian and Tyrus, the milk jug swinging by his side, the lancet in his hand. He sat Emalie on the street and knelt down, placing the jug beside her. The onlookers were quiet as he whispered unintelligible demon words, then pressed the lancet into the hole in her neck. The blood began to flow back in, making a sound like a sucking straw.

A pale light appeared, and Oliver found Nathan and Emalie's soul beside him. *Hey*, said Nathan.

"Is that your . . ." Phlox began, staring at Nathan, wide-eyed.

"My soul," said Oliver. "Yeah." Oliver watched Phlox's face, worried what she might think, but he couldn't tell from her blank expression.

Emalie's skin began to warm.

It was nice meeting you, Nathan said as Emalie's soul was slowly pulled from beside him. It rose above Emalie's chest and began to sink back into her, just below her neck. Now Oliver caught the faintest scent from her, and when she took her first big breath, he felt a burst of relief.

"You okay?" he asked.

"Think so," she said groggily, getting to her feet. Then she turned. "Mom," she whispered, and burst into tears. Margaret wrapped her arms around her.

"Pleasant nights, everyone," said Sylvix politely, and left.

"How did you do that?" Phlox asked Margaret, her tone respectful. "How did you fend off Désirée and free us from that place?"

Margaret spoke as much to Emalie as to the rest of the group. "While I've been gone, I learned the source of Orani power. Our bloodline traces further back than anyone knew. We're descendants of the Architects. And in a very few of us, that original power, that direct link to the Architects, is turned on. It's like a dormant gene. . . ."

"An Artifact," Sebastian added.

"Yes, it's turned on in me. And it's turned on in my daughter." She looked to Emalie with fresh tears. "I had to run, to disappear, because Half-Light was after me. They wanted to use my power to Anoint Oliver, only they'd misread the prophecy. You were the one, Emalie. If only I had seen it, I could have taken you with me."

"It's okay, Mom," said Emalie.

"But it's not," said Margaret. "Désirée and Half-Light will be after you both now."

"We can handle Half-Light," said Phlox. "And you fought Désirée off with that mirror."

"I did, but only because I surprised her. I delivered a message from the other Architects."

"You've spoken to them?" Sebastian asked in awe.

"Yes," said Margaret. "After the Architects built the worlds and closed the Gate, they didn't leave. They each took trust of the world that they'd done the most work to build, to oversee its function. Désirée is Earth's Architect, but she's become deranged, damaged by the effects of Finity. The other Architects wanted her to understand that they disapprove of her actions."

"Will that stop her?" asked Dean.

Margaret shook her head. "I doubt it."

Silence passed over the group.

Finally, Oliver asked, "Emalie, was that really Bane? Was he . . . with you?"

Emalie nodded. "Yeah . . . his *vampyr* . . . It was with me all this time, hiding. I didn't really know it was there, but maybe I kinda did. I mean, I think he was helping me with my powers. . . . And waiting. Like he knew there'd be a chance to avenge his slaying."

"How is that possible?" Phlox asked, listening intently.

"Well, we'd worked together before," Emalie added absently. "Feels kinda empty without him now, actually."

"Oh, dear," said Margaret, her face tight with concern. "This is worse than I feared."

"I'm okay, Mom," said Emalie, but she still sounded weak. Then she looked to Oliver. "We didn't stop the Anointment."

"No," said Oliver. He gazed down the street and felt a great sinking feeling inside. He couldn't rejoin his soul anymore. And worse, here he was, so close to his human parents, but . . . how could he meet them, knowing his prophecy would destroy them? "Why did you bring us here?" he asked Margaret.

"Because there's another chance," she replied. "The Architects told us of another way to stop the prophecy. Selene left it in your parents' house, just in case."

"Another chance?" Oliver echoed.

"Yes," said Margaret. "It's in there. In the crib."

"The crib?" Oliver asked.

"You'll understand after," said Margaret.

Come on, said Nathan, starting off.

Oliver hesitated. He was so close, and he wanted to go so badly . . . but he looked worriedly back at his vampire parents.

"Go," said Phlox. "Find whatever is there for you."

Oliver turned, but couldn't quite make his feet move. Then he felt warmth on his back. *Sun!* He turned to see its glowing orange rim rising just over the horizon.

"We'd better find some cover," said Tyrus, moving out of the road.

"Hurry, Ollie," said Sebastian.

Oliver looked to Emalie. She nodded and started down the street beside him. They walked quickly. The dangerous warmth of the rising sun made Oliver's skin prickle.

Ahead, Nathan stood at the edge of a driveway where the road began to curve. The mailbox read 714. They followed him toward the front porch. Oliver was surprised to see a red tricycle on the little brick walkway. They reached a screen door, and a white door behind that. Nathan passed through it. The white door swung open.

Oliver felt frozen. His nerves were vibrating like cello strings. It was all he could do just to stand here. He had wanted to find his parents for so long, and yet, he hadn't actually considered what he was going to *do* when he found them. Should he just introduce himself? *But I'm a vampire. I might terrify them.*

You can do it, thought Emalie, and gave him a gentle push through the door.

Inside was a long living room attached to a dining room, and a small kitchen around a corner. The house was recently built and yet the furniture was old, antique. Faint morning light filtered through blinds.

Where are you? Oliver called to Nathan.

I'm right here.

"Oliver," Emalie whispered. "You're glowing."

Oliver looked down. A white glow radiated off his body, blue sparks around its edges.

We can be together here, said Nathan.

Oliver couldn't believe the feeling. Like there was more to him. Not like he was whole, because he could feel that Nathan was separate, but at the same time, it was like Nathan filled in certain spaces, made spots solid that he hadn't even noticed were hollow, and made things calm. It gave Oliver an incredible sense of relief.

Over here. Oliver and Nathan walked to the television. Above it was a shelf, lined with photos. Emalie joined them, taking their hands.

Oliver spied a black-and-white photo of Howard and Lindsey. They looked just as they had on the night he'd been sired, their faces smooth, young. Howard was handsome, and wearing a military uniform in the photo, his arm around Lindsey, who wore a polka-dot dress and Howard's pointed hat. They were grinning at the camera, a party in full swing behind them. The tarnished silver frame was engraved: *V-J DAY, 1945*. Oliver touched the photo. Imagining them as his parents. Imagining living here . . .

Yet there were more photos on either side. Oliver found a blurry color photo of his parents in casual clothes — with a new baby. A girl, wrapped in a pink blanket . . .

Then Howard and Lindsey and that girl on a motorboat, on a lake in the sun. Howard with thick sideburns, and the girl, maybe five, with long dark hair, the color of Lindsey's and Oliver's . . .

That's Adelaide, said Nathan.

"Their daughter?" asked Oliver.

Yes. And our sister.

Of course it was. Still, Oliver felt a lump growing in his throat.

The pictures went on. . . . Their arms around Adelaide, who wore a black graduation cap and gown. She had on purple tinted glasses and was making a peace sign at the camera. . . .

Then Adelaide in a skirt, standing among villagers in dry, thirsty countryside . . .

Then in a beautiful white dress, with a smiling, bearded man . . .

Then with a baby of her own . . .

Steven.

Looking down the mantle, Oliver saw Steven grow up, too, from baby to toddler to young soccer player in the afternoon sun, to college graduate, to groom. And Oliver's sister went from young woman to older, her hair lightening to gray. All in Oliver's short existence . . .

This way. They turned toward the hallway.

"I'll wait here," whispered Emalie.

The hall was short, ending at three doorways. The one to the left was open slightly. Oliver spectralized, and entered.

Howard and Lindsey were in the bed, Howard snoring, his mouth half-open, Lindsey's breath slow and frail. Their hair was white.

Oliver stepped close to the bed, looking down at his mother's face. Her nose was more curved. It had lost the perfect straightness from its photos. Her cheeks had sunk, and looked hollow.

They're so old, he and Nathan thought together. It made him sad in a way he couldn't describe. He wanted them to be the young, smiling faces in the old photos. Wanted them to have their lives ahead of them. They would be gone soon, these parents of his, and there was nothing to be done.

Lindsey stirred, and suddenly sat up with such speed that Oliver had to leap backward. He bumped the wall. Lindsey turned. Oliver pressed back, spectralizing as hard as he could.

Lindsey's wrinkled eyes peered in Oliver's direction. She looked frightened. "Nathan?" she whispered.

Mom, Oliver and Nathan thought. *We should say hello*, thought Oliver. *Tell her it's okay —*

"Gam Gam?"

A very young boy stood in the doorway, wearing blue pajamas.

Lindsey blinked, then reached to the nightstand with shaking fingers. She picked up her glasses and slipped them on. "Oh, Peter," she said.

"Who you talking to, Gam Gam?" Peter asked. He glanced in Oliver's direction.

"Who —" Lindsey looked perplexed, and a shadow crossed her face.

"Was it a ghost?" Peter asked. "Ghosts are scary."

"No, no, Peter, it wasn't a ghost. . . . It was just a dream. An old dream." Lindsey glanced warily toward Oliver again. "Go back to bed, sugar."

"'Kay." Peter turned and walked off.

Lindsey pulled off her glasses and lay back down, rolling over with her back to Oliver. She sighed deeply.

Oliver backed out of the room. He just wanted to leave. He didn't want to be the ghost, the old, frightening dream. He didn't want his parents to be so frail, didn't want them to have other kids, grandkids, *great*-grandkids. He wanted to be their son, and them to be young. . . . He wondered if it had been a mistake to come here.

But Nathan turned him into the next room. *Come on*, he urged. Staying spectralized, Oliver entered a small room, its floor cluttered with toys, most of which were dinosaurs. Peter was busy getting back into a tiny bed and pulling up the covers.

On the other side of the room stood a white crib filled with stuffed animals. Oliver approached, and his gaze fell on the mobile hanging above it. It looked very old. The little circus animals hanging from it were made of wood, hand-painted. There was a simple windup mechanism in a round box in the center, with a silver key. Oliver pulled the box toward him and saw the hand-carved inscription in it:

TO NATHAN, 12-28-45

Though it seemed impossible, Oliver swore he could remember it, could remember gazing up at the spinning animals with wide, innocent eyes, so long ago. He wanted to wind it up and hear it sing —

That's what I always want, too. But we can't. We'd wake everybody.

Oliver felt that horrible, pressing ball in his throat grow beyond control, like it would burst out the back of his neck, or his chest, and then he hunched, sucking in air, and for the second time in his existence, he wept.

I miss them, he and Nathan thought as one. *Can I miss them without even knowing them?*

Tears fell onto the animals.

"Why you crying?"

Oliver turned to see Peter sitting up in bed, gazing at him seriously. And Oliver realized that he'd let himself reappear in the room.

"I don't really know," said Oliver honestly.

"Maybe it's 'cause you have an owwie," said Peter. "I fell down and had to get a Band-Aid." Peter bent his elbow toward Oliver, pointing at a bandage with pictures of a big red dog. Peter frowned. "I wanted to put it on my own."

"Peter?" The voice came from the door. "Who are you talking to?" A woman appeared in the doorway. Gray tousled hair, wearing sweatpants and a sweatshirt. She looked toward Oliver, but he had spectralized once more. Still, her gaze lingered.

Peter looked back at where Oliver had been, frowned, and turned to Adelaide, Oliver's sister, now an older woman herself. "Gramma, I showed dat boy my owwie," he reported.

Adelaide nodded. "Right, you mean at the park yesterday."

"No, the ghost. Over dere." He pointed toward the crib.

Adelaide peered in Oliver's direction again, and Oliver felt sure that though she couldn't see him, she sensed him — sensed *something*.

They know, thought Oliver. *Somewhere inside, they all know.*

Adelaide's mouth tightened. Oliver detected a trace of fear in her scent. Yet she turned back to Peter and whispered tenderly, "There are no ghosts, honey."

"Okay," Peter said, disappointed. He sat on his bed. "I miss Mommy and Daddy."

Adelaide sat with Peter. "They miss you, too, honey. But they went on a cruise for their anniversary because they love each other, and they'll be back very soon. And they'll be so happy to see you." She glanced at the window, and then toward Oliver again. "You know, it's morning now, want to go mark your calendar?"

"'Kay."

"Get your blankie and your friends." She shuffled out.

Peter gathered an armful of stuffed animals and a worn yellow blanket decorated with little sea creatures. Oliver recognized it from the Portal. It had once been wrapped around him.

In the crib, said Nathan. Oliver turned back to the crib and reached down among the stuffed animals. Pushing them carefully aside, he spied another amethyst box, its top engraved with a Skrit symbol he didn't recognize:

He put it in his sweatshirt pocket. After a last look at
the mobile, he turned to leave.

Peter turned from his bed, having added a plastic dinner plate to his armful of animals. "Bye, ghost," he
whispered, even though Oliver was still spectralized.

Oliver and Nathan stopped, having a thought together.
Oliver remembered Jenette, the wraiths on the beach,
Lindsey's frightened eyes, and allowed himself to reappear, glowing with Nathan's light. "There *are* ghosts,"
said Oliver. "But they aren't scary. We watch over you,
to keep you safe." He ruffled Peter's hair, then left
the room.

Oliver stopped in the hall, watching as Peter found
Adelaide in the third bedroom. She was holding a calendar, and a Magic Marker.

"Where do I draw?" Peter asked.

"Right here," said Adelaide. "Today is the twenty-first. Let's draw a smiley face, and then look, only one more day till Mommy and Daddy come home."

Oliver returned to the living room. Emalie was waiting. Margaret had joined them. Sunlight streamed through the gaps in the blinds.

"I already took your parents and Dean back," she said, and held out her hands.

Oliver, Emalie, and Margaret joined hands. As the room began to fade, Oliver looked at Emalie. She smiled at him, but he couldn't quite return it. He didn't totally understand what had just happened . . . didn't know if he would understand it for a long time. He glanced around his parents' house, feeling an urge to stay, despite how he'd wanted to leave. . . .

And now he felt himself and Nathan separating. There was a moment of stretching, like things were pulling apart that shouldn't. *Don't —*

Have to, said Nathan. *Someday we'll come back. . . .*

The quiet house in the desert faded from sight.

CHAPTER 15

The Triad of Finity

Oliver looked around to find them in, of all places, Dean's living room. It was still predawn in the northern latitudes, the sky purple.

"This is good," Sebastian observed. "It's not the first place Half-Light would check, so we should have a little time before they find us."

Tammy nearly collapsed at the sight of them all, but then recovered and set to work furiously scooping out leftovers and even offing one of the chickens with what was becoming expert efficiency. The sound of the cleaver woke Kyle, Elizabeth, and Mitch, who all crowded into the living room as well.

"No way," said Kyle, spying Phlox and Sebastian, who sat stiffly on a love seat, their backs straight. "*Real* vampires! Can you guys do the cool stuff that *he* can't?"

"Thanks," Oliver groaned.

"Kyle David!" Tammy scolded as she handed small juice glasses to Phlox and Sebastian. "Sorry I don't have any . . . um, people blood," said Tammy apologetically.

"This will be fine," said Sebastian, and then managed to add, "You're a very gracious host."

Dean, Oliver, and Emalie shared a smile.

There was a knock at the door. Dean opened it to find Aunt Kathleen. She rushed in, embracing Margaret. "Oh, dear, it's so good to see you again."

Oliver, the message, said Nathan, from the corner.

"Oh, yeah." Oliver removed the amethyst box carefully from his pocket. He opened it to find another still firefly. Nathan pinched himself, and put the drop of glowing white on the insect. It buzzed to life, shimmering green and hovering above his hand, captivating the room.

Oliver, said Selene's ghostly voice, *if you get this message, then the Anointment has been successful, and the chance to undo your prophecy as I instructed has passed. . . . But, though the road will now be harder, the Architects have built another safeguard into the universe, as a means of protecting the Gate.*

There exist three elements, known as the Triad of Finity. They are most cleverly hidden. If you possess the Triad when Illisius summons you and Emalie to the Gate, then you will have a chance to resist opening it. Collect the Triad, Oliver. You will know how to find them when the first speaks to you. Be well . . .

The firefly went dark and fell to the floor, where it lay still.

The room was silent. Finally, Dean spoke up. "Sounds like we have our next assignment." Another quiet moment passed. "Okay . . . sounds like we need kidney pie and ice cream first."

There was a knock on the door.

"Margaret," said Tammy, nodding toward the door.

Margaret's eyes grew wide, immediately leaking tears. She got up and opened the door. Cole stood outside, his eyes wet as well. They rushed into each other's arms. "I'm so sorry," Margaret said into his shoulder. "I'll explain everything." She turned back. "Emalie, come out here."

Emalie, watching her parents' reunion with tear-filled awe, got up and joined them. The Watkins moved out onto the porch, closing the door behind them.

Oliver looked to Phlox and Sebastian, wondering worriedly what their reaction would be to the message from Selene. They had saved him, had learned of his soul, his human parents, all in such a short time. How would they take all this?

Sebastian met his gaze. "We'll have to go to great lengths," he said grimly, "to hide this plan from Half-Light."

Oliver gazed at him in surprise.

Sebastian went on, businesslike. "You are more

important than ever to Half-Light. The Anointment was a success, albeit not what they planned for. Which means that there cannot be another attempt at the prophecy. You and Emalie are truly Half-Light's last hope to open the Gate."

"And the world's last hope to keep it closed," said Aunt Kathleen.

"Half-Light will keep a tighter reign on us than ever," said Phlox. "It will be difficult to deceive them."

"But," said Oliver, "we can try? You guys are okay with . . . ending the prophecy?"

Sebastian took Phlox's hand. "Myrandah is going to be in her glory about this," he murmured to her.

Phlox sighed. "And I'll have to double my efforts against global warming, if in fact we won't be leaving this world." She smiled at Oliver.

Oliver looked at them, his parents, and smiled, too.

"Ice cream time," said Dean, returning with an armful of bowls, along with a plate of maroon-colored pie for himself.

"I have a blood sauce," said Tammy, getting up and heading for the kitchen, "but it's only pig."

"Do you have any dark chocolate?" Phlox asked, getting up to join her. "That, with some cayenne and the venom sac of a pit viper, makes an excellent topping."

"I — I don't have any viper sac thingies," said Tammy, "but I have the rest."

"That will do," said Phlox. "I'll show you the best method for combining them."

Oliver watched, amazed, and tried to share another incredulous smile with Dean, but Dean was gazing at the front door, where Emalie stood, Margaret and Cole behind her.

Emalie's eyes were red and puffy, her expression tragic. Margaret and Cole didn't look happy, either.

"Hey," said Dean, "what's up?"

"I'm sorry, everyone," said Margaret, glancing uncomfortably around the room, "but we have to be going."

"Oh, heading home so soon?" asked Tammy, hurrying back into the room with Phlox.

"We're . . . not heading home, exactly," said Margaret. Emalie turned and pushed through them, storming out of sight. "Emalie . . ." Margaret called after her.

"Come on," said Dean, passing Oliver. The two ducked around Margaret and Cole, out the door.

They found Emalie on the roof, face in her hands, sobbing. The early morning sky had brightened, but luckily a layer of low clouds kept the light gloomy.

"What is it?" asked Dean. He and Oliver sat on either side of her.

"We're leaving," Emalie muttered into her hands.

"Leaving for where?" asked Oliver nervously.

"We're going to Arcana."

"Arcana?" Dean asked. "Didn't that place burn down, like, over a hundred years ago?"

"Yes," said Emalie.

Oliver remembered that photo in Fortuna, and felt his insides dropping away. "She's taking you back in time."

"It's the only way to keep her safe." Margaret had appeared on the roof, using the same trick of levitating that Emalie knew.

"I'll be safe here!" Emalie shouted, glaring at her.

"No," said Margaret softly, "you won't."

"But," Oliver tried desperately, "you heard Selene, we have to go to the Gate together —"

"Emalie is not going to *survive* to go to the Gate with you if she stays here," said Margaret. "Her powers are beyond anyone's understanding. We need to figure out how she melded with Bane's demon, and what it means that she was Anointed, and we need to do it some-where safe."

Oliver saw the sense in what Margaret was saying. And he remembered Emalie at the Ball, with her dead skin, and how strange and dangerous she had acted with a demon inside. "But —" he began anyway.

"Look, I know you both mean well," Margaret said to Oliver and Dean. "But things have changed. Every powerful being in the universe will have felt tonight's

Anointment. There are those who will want to control Emalie's power. It's an old story for the Orani. Who's going to protect her when the powerful come for her?"

"We could," said Oliver.

"I'm sorry," said Margaret. "She's already been in enough danger with you."

Oliver didn't argue that point.

"I did fine," Emalie huffed.

"Emalie," said Margaret sternly. She looked to Oliver again. "We'll keep in touch with your parents about our progress."

Oliver tried to think of some other argument for making her stay, but then realized that Dean had not been protesting. And neither had Emalie, despite her tears. Knowing her, if she really didn't want something, she'd fight much harder than this to avoid it.

"How long?" Oliver asked simply.

"I don't know," said Margaret. "As long as it takes."

"Margie," Cole called from below. "Kathleen left. She's meeting us at the house."

"Okay," said Margaret. "Emalie, take a minute." She blinked out of sight.

"Emalie . . ." Oliver began.

"She's right," said Emalie, lifting her face from her hands.

Oliver tried to think of something to say, but what? He felt a small tickle on his hand, and looked down to see Emalie's creeping into his. She squeezed his hand so tightly . . .

Then stood up. "No big good-byes," she said, staring at the ground. "See ya, cousin."

Dean stood and they hugged. "We'll miss you, Em," he said quietly. "Don't be gone long."

Emalie pulled away, fresh tears falling. "You bet."

Oliver stood, shivering, almost falling over. He took a hesitant step toward her —

But Emalie backed away. She fiddled in her bag and pulled out her camera, the one Oliver had given her. She aimed it at him, doing her best to twist the lens with shaking fingers.

"But —" Oliver began. Had she forgotten that he would just appear blurry in a photograph?

"Sshh." She twisted the focus and snapped the shutter. When she lowered the camera, her eyes were overflowing. "I know what you look like."

"Emalie," Margaret called urgently from below. "We need to go, now."

Oliver tried to make his voice work, but it wouldn't.

Emalie nodded to herself. "Bye, guys," she whispered. She turned to go —

Then darted back and kissed Oliver on the lips.

Afterward, Oliver would replay the moment a million times in his head and wonder, why did he just stand there like an idiot? Why didn't he kiss back? Why didn't he throw his arms around her and hug her so tight that her scent would seep into his skin and never, ever leave? Why didn't he tell her that she needed to stay, *he* needed her to stay more than he'd ever needed anything before —

But in the moment, it was all he could do to keep track of who he was and where he was standing. Oliver felt like a bolt of lightning had struck him in the chest, only it stayed impaled there, and as Emalie pulled away, turning her tear-streaked face and starting down the roof, Oliver felt like the bolt was being ripped back out of him, each sharp edge tearing him open further, making a wound that would never heal. *Don't . . . go . . .*

Emalie flashed a final smile in their direction, and winked out of sight.

"Bye," said Oliver weakly.

There was no reply in the night.

A hand slapped him on the shoulder. "Come on, killer," said Dean, pointing toward the lightening sky. "You'll see her again."

Oliver was glad that Dean hadn't bothered to lie and say anything like, *it will be okay . . .* because this was not okay. And yet, Dean was right. He would see Emalie again. Not because of some prophecy, or Gate.

But simply because he *had* to.

Chapter 16

Hope

Oliver Nocturne had been having trouble sleeping, which was why he heard the intruder.

Hey, it called weakly.

Oliver dropped his video game and quietly opened his coffin, glad to be distracted from the thoughts that plagued him. He'd always had trouble sleeping around his birthday and Christmas, both of which were coming up. This year wasn't worse than ever, but it wasn't any better, either.

He slipped upstairs, silent except for the persistent light clinking of metal that now followed him everywhere he went. He passed the kitchen, climbing to the steel door above, and paused. He reached up into the boards and unplugged the closed-circuit cameras, which now fed directly to Half-Light, then opened the door. He ducked around the broken, rusted refrigerator, and crossed the room, past the grimy bathtub, to where an old mattress lay on the floor, just beyond the reach of gray daylight through the broken windows.

Sitting on it, back against the wall, legs stretched out, was Oliver's ghostly white soul.

Hey, said Oliver, sitting down beside Nathan. He felt the calming, warm presence beside him, the prickle of sparks falling on his skin, but he longed for that sense of completion, of empty corners being filled inside him as he'd felt when they joined. Still, this was better than nothing.

Anything on the Triad? Nathan asked.

Nothing. Selene said it would come to me, but —

Then it will.

I don't want to wait.

I know.

Oliver leaned his head back against the wall.

She'll come back, Nathan said a moment later.

Oliver pictured Emalie on the roof . . . and hated himself for letting her go. *Maybe.*

Soon, he drifted off to sleep.

✹

He awoke to find evening streetlight filtering through the windows. Nathan was gone. His visits were short, to keep Half-Light from finding him. Oliver shuffled back to the door, reattached the cameras, and headed downstairs toward his coffin.

"Oliver."

He turned to find Phlox and Sebastian sitting at the kitchen island, sipping coffee.

"Couldn't sleep?" Phlox asked.

"No," Oliver said.

"Well then." Phlox reached to the counter. "Have some frosting." She slid a crystal bowl of whipped fudge frosting to the empty seat at the island.

"Okay." Oliver sat and dug into the sugary dish. After a couple bites, he looked up to find Phlox peering at him. "What?"

She glanced up at the ceiling, then back to him, and nodded.

Oliver nodded back. Half-Light had bugged the house with listening devices. The Nocturnes hadn't objected, knowing it would do no good. Now they just had to be careful.

"We're having the cousins over for Longest Night," said Phlox, eating from her own bowl of frosting. "I've invited the Aunders as well."

"Cool," Oliver replied.

"I should get to the office," said Sebastian. As he stood, there was another clinking of metal. On his ankle was a thin silver ring: a tracking device. Phlox and Oliver had them as well. If any of them tried to go somewhere other than school, work, or Central Council, the anklet notified Half-Light. Trips to the Underground, even Harvey's, required escorts. "Have a good night at school, Ollie," said Sebastian, rubbing Oliver's hair as he swept out of the room.

Oliver finished his breakfast. As he readied for school, his thoughts drifted. Would tonight be the night? Would he learn something of the Triad of Finity? Or ... *Will she come back?*

Emalie ...

The answer to both questions was likely no, and yet, as Oliver slung his heavy backpack over his shoulder, put up his sweatshirt hood, and emerged from a sewer tunnel into a night of cold, steady rain, his slight smile formed for just a moment.

It probably wouldn't happen, but it *might*. Oliver felt that little surge of nervous energy, the one that a year ago he wouldn't have understood, but that now he was lucky enough to know:

It was hope.

Discover the world on the
other side of night...

Meet

OLIVER
NOCTURNE

He's not your typical vampire.

#1: THE VAMPIRE'S PHOTOGRAPH

#2: THE SUNLIGHT SLAYINGS

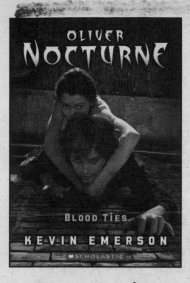

#3: Blood Ties

#4: The Demon Hunter

#5: The Eternal Tomb

Could the road to the afterlife
be a two-way street?

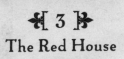

{ 1 }
City of the Dead

{ 2 }
Bayou Dogs

{ 3 }
The Red House